Meet me in Red Bank: The Awakening

Dedicated to my dear parents,

Mrs. Girija Bala & Mr. Venkata Subba Rao Achyuthuni

Author's Note

On Christmas Day of 2002, God placed me in the delightful town of Red Bank, in Monmouth County, New Jersey. Fresh snowfall, deserted streets and a superb Sony DSC-707 digital camera in my backpack led to the photo that is on the cover of this book, *Meet me in Red Bank - The Awakening*.

This book started out as an online soap opera before it morphed into a novel. As always, there are a number of good friends and teachers who have helped me give life to the characters in my works of fiction.

Meet me in Red Bank was written as a trilogy, with *The Awakening* as the first volume; the second volume is still to be completed, and interestingly the last volume is close to its finish.

Many distractions, normal and otherwise, such as starting and finishing two other works of fiction (*Living out of a Tin Cup* and *Fear*), delayed its release. In contrast, *Living out of a Tin Cup* went from thought to print in a month; many have asked if I have any plans for a sequel to that short novella, but regretfully I don't.

I worked very hard to create this book, which is available for sale in print and as an electronic book in all the usual places. My thanks to Ms. Karen Faiella, my creative editor.

Bhaskara Rao Achyuthuni

March 2013

For more information, please contact the publisher:

Magai New Media, LLC

P.O. Box 740

Rumson, NJ 07760-0740

www.magai.com

The Awakening

3:00 a.m., Sunday January 6, 2002. Navesink River, Middletown, New Jersey.

Tara Morgan woke up long before the alarm clock. It was not the broad, crisp waterfall of moonlight cascading from the French doors onto the wooden floor that broke her sleep; it was not even her parched mouth dry as the sands of Sandy Hook, a few miles to the northeast as the crow flies from the secluded estates of the Navesink section of Middletown, New Jersey. It was a deep queasiness, a foreboding of the days that lay ahead.

After taking a carefully measured swallow of water, for she did not want to get up later to answer nature's call, she swung her legs off the bed and eased herself into the rocking chair, one that had seen many a long night comforting her daughter Jamie, a precocious five-going-on-six-hurriedly, who was fast asleep in her own room across from the landing.

Tara drew a quilt across herself, squirmed to settle back into the long spindles, and gazed blankly out the French doors at the Navesink River that flowed past her house. In the rippled waters she could see the reflection of the

1

moon. She distinctly recalled Jamie observing one evening, *Mommy, even when you can't see the entire moon, it is still there. You can't always believe what you see. You have to know.*

Almost a mile away, separated by the cold, choppy waters of the Navesink Basin, the lights of Red Bank twinkled back at her from the south bank. A slender finger of a floating dock, seldomly used since they had never owned a boat, bobbed and twitched on a patch of slurried ice.

Once in a dozen or so winters the river froze enough for wooden iceboats to race. Historians had noted that in the early nineteen hundreds this was quite a common occurrence, but not so in the dawn of the new millennium.

The two-story house lay nestled on a level plot of about two acres. The semi-circular driveway, fashioned of gravel as was customary in her neck of the woods, was now almost white with the remnants of the last big snowfall. Outside, the north winds whistled and shrieked as they parted ways with the cold Atlantic at the Sandy Hook National Preserve and fiercely came down the hills of Locust. They continued southward to rattle the house as they had for well over three decades.

Her late father William James Morgan III, who was not even an architect, had designed the house which was built just before Tara was born. His directions to first-time visitors had always drawn disbelief, "We are in the house with no windows." *How could that be*, people would ask. Technically her father was right, for the house had only French doors with true divided light so that the entire house could be opened up to the elements during the spring, summer and fall.

Covered verandahs wrapped around both stories of the house, liberally sprinkled with rockers, occasional tables and wooden chaise lounges, and punctuated by planters, both of the hanging and stationary types.

About a hundred yards away to the left, a stone and wood gazebo stood in a clearing close to the riverbank. It was empty now, but that was where her mother, attended by their Alsatian guard dogs, spent a portion of her day.

During the winter, deer frequently ventured out of the woods, driven by sheer hunger, and even dared to come right up to the house, undeterred by the Alsatians that had been trained to not bother them. So they came, and freely shredded most of her foundation plants. That did not bother Tara much, for she reasoned that they had as valid a claim on her land as she did, and ultimately had nowhere else to go, since dwellings such as hers rudely encroached on their natural foraging grounds. Yet, she did not attempt to provide food for them, since that would domicile them, and ruin their natural instincts. Besides, they did harbor ticks that could bear the dreaded Lyme Disease.

In the sharp light of the full moon, a "fine hunting moon" as her father had always called it even though he himself had never hunted animals, she could almost see every individual round pebble in the walkway that led to the gazebo. There were no deer milling around the clearing, and she was glad, for the sight of any creature out in that deep cold would surely upset her.

Tara was no stranger to these disturbed nights, and as always haunting memories of her father accompanied her solitude. Her eyes grew moist, and the tears flooded her eyes and ran down her cheeks. She made no attempt to wipe them until the congestion in her nose became unbearable. Failing to find a box of tissues within reach, she wiped her face on the sleeve of her flannel pajamas.

കാ കാ കാ കാ കാ

Tara woke up again, this time under the intense scrutiny of the greenest eyes ever, framed by a shock of curly blonde hair, with a cute pug nose. Jamie stood there, dressed in a cream-colored wool dress with a pattern of soft green periwinkle, and shod in tasseled white socks and brown Mary

Janes. Bright, cleansing sunlight had chased away all the demons of the dark night, and Tara sighed in relief.

"Mommy, Nana said that unless you get up, we are going to be late for church, and we will have to speed, and still be late, and not find a place to sit that's not way out in the back!" Nana was Isabella Morgan, Tara's mother. "You are not going back to sleep again, are you, Mommy?" Usually her first entreaties were to play cards or a board game, but she knew the routine on Sundays. Going to church was mandatory.

"Not with you around, you! Give me a hug!" But in place of the usual ferocious leap into her arms, Jamie reached up on tiptoes and wrapped her arms around Tara's neck, and hung on tight. A cold, wet nose nuzzled against her mother's warm shoulder. Tara reciprocated; she inhaled deeply of her daughter's inviting warmth, and nibbled playfully on her ear. With a small squeal, the tight seal was broken.

Her mother Isabella, nee Schoen, had been widowed at 40, when Tara herself was only 15; William James Morgan III, Tara's father, was buried in a closed casket. It was only after the funeral that Tara had learned the truth, not from her mother, not from the hospital to which his lifeless body had been taken, not from the priest and certainly not from the countless eulogies, but instead from one of her schoolmates, who had said "I'm sorry your father shot himself."

While Jamie nibbled on a thick slice of homemade country bread slathered with seedless raspberry marmalade and washed it down with soy milk, Tara showered quickly. Still somewhat damp, she rummaged through the armoire of crisp haute couture dresses and suits that had lain dormant since September 11, 2001. On that gruesome day, still less than four months ago, hearts had gone cold, minds went numb and time stood frozen, as the hopes, dreams and lives of many thousands came to an untimely, abrupt halt with the four hijacked jet airplanes that had been deliberately crashed. Middletown, New Jersey, its profound but not unique sadness immortalized in Gail Sheehy's documentary book, had suffered the most lost, especially in the fallen Twin Towers.

With a deep sigh, Tara picked a simple, navy-blue woolen pleated skirt and a snug waist-length dark green woolen jacket worn over an off-white silk blouse that buttoned all the way to a close neck. Jackie Kennedy could have worn it in the Camelot White House. To alleviate an impingement in her right shoulder, Tara had recently undergone arthroscopic surgery, which once again made it somewhat possible to raise her arm above her shoulders, and to reach her own back. The surgery had left three little puncture wounds on the round of her shoulder. Jamie called them vampire bites.

A single gold-clasped strand of white pearls provided a sharp visual break. A small mechanical wind-up gold Swiss watch with a black leather band, given to her as a high-school graduation present by her mother, was the only additional jewelry. Until a fateful day less than six months prior, an elegant diamond ring had adorned her left hand, as had a gold wedding band.

Her dark, straight, long brown hair stopped just short of her shoulders, and equally dark brown eyebrows, discreetly plucked, framed her own green eyes. Tara usually did not wear any makeup during the day, especially not to church, and not even to cover a small but permanent scar above her right eyebrow, and another one above her upper lip.

Jamie was waiting for her at the bottom of the stairs, and handed her a travel mug. Tara smiled, "Thanks for the tea, Jamie! Give me a big hug and a kiss. *Mmm*, my favorite, raspberry marmalade kisses! Here, let me lick it off." Tara rubbed Jamie's grateful back, and kissed her tousled head. "Nana will drive us. Right, Nana?"

Isabella Morgan merely put on her sunglasses and shepherded Jamie out the door into the icy cold, and to the detached carriage house where a dark green Range Rover was parked alongside a champagne-colored Porsche 911 Turbo. Tara carefully placed her travel mug on the roof as she helped Jamie buckle up, and then climbed into the front.

As the Range Rover lurched out of the carriage house, she heard the crash of the mug sliding off the roof where she had forgotten it, followed by a perversely satisfying squish as the rear wheel ran over it. "I just hope today's Doughnut Sunday at the church."

They turned west onto Cooper's Avenue, which wound its way along the north shore of the Navesink River, passing a wide variety of houses, ranging from breathtaking mansions to modest bungalows. A mile later, they turned south onto State Highway 35 that ran through the eastern seaboard of Monmouth County, and changed names in Red Bank alone to Broad Street, Maple Avenue, Front Street, Water Street, Pearl Street, Riverside Avenue, Prospect Place, Bridge Street, Cooper's Bridge, amongst many other names as it traversed through many other towns. Highway 35, by any name, took them over the new Cooper's Bridge that connected the Township of Middletown to the Borough of Red Bank.

ↇ ↇ ↇ ↇ ↇ

The electronic bells in the steeple of St. James' Roman Catholic Church, prominent in the movie 'Dogma', pealed their Sunday morning call to the faithful as they parked the Range Rover on Broad Street and walked in. At the main entrance, they stopped to dip their fingers in the Holy Water, which represented their own baptism. Tara watched Jamie bring together the thumb, forefinger and index finger of her right hand. Then she touched the fingers to her forehead, breast, left shoulder and lastly the right shoulder. Once in a while, Jamie went right to left instead, which, being the preferred practice of Eastern Catholics, was not wrong in itself.

They were fortunate to get the end of a pew, and had barely a brief moment to bow before Father Clancy began the Mass with the Trinitarian exalt, sung *a capella*, "In the name of the Father, and of the Son, and of the Holy Spirit".

With a responding Amen, Tara was finally able to take a deep, calming breath to shake off the stress of getting to the church on time to celebrate the Eucharist. She took it very seriously, since this sacrament, in Catholic doctrine, was the manifestation of the Sacrifice of Christ.

Everything that she knew about being a Catholic, she had learned from her father. He had been involved in hand-to-hand mortal combat in Vietnam, and had returned quite moved, attributing his mental and physical survival to his gradual acceptance of a benevolent Benefactor represented by a small gold cross that he wore around his neck at the urging of a chaplain.

In the pew directly in front of her, a newly minted young mother fussed unnecessarily with the pink knit bonnet of a tiny baby draped over her proud father's shoulder; her eyes tightly shut, she was hardly a month old judging from the peeling skin.

"Mommy, look! A brand new baby," whispered Jamie excitedly, tugging at Tara's skirt. The mother, not much over twenty, if even that, turned around and smiled knowingly at Jamie and mouthed a silent *hi* to Tara. She wore black slacks, a white turtleneck, and a fitted dark brown leather jacket. Her nails were an even crimson all around. Her layered blond hair came down to her shoulders, and an oversized ostrich leather bag lay next to a starkly incongruent unblemished diaper bag. Her husband was dressed in almost exactly the same outfit, and his auburn hair was cut crisply close to his head. Tara shook her head. *Amazing what a measly five years or even the wrong 5 seconds can do to change your life.*

Hearing the congregation sing the refrain of *Kyrie* - Lord have Mercy, Christ have Mercy, Lord have Mercy - she realized that she had missed reciting the *Mea Culpa*. By itself, this recital did not procure absolution; that came only through a confession, as part of the Sacrament of Penance. She had a clear conscience, having confessed, not for the first time, to the Father Confessor, thankfully separated by a curtain of privacy, that yes, she had sinned. She was quite specific about the sins that she had committed. These were the usual ones; she had lied on occasion, expressed anger at others, taken God's name in vain, committed various acts of sloth, and she had pleasured herself.

The priest had made sure that she expressed sincere contrition, which she had, and had prescribed acts of penance, which she had executed, thus acquiring absolution. So, unlike a holy pretender, of which she knew there surely were quite a few amongst the congregation, she could walk up and partake of the Communion with full innocence.

Father Clancy had a choice of hymns, and much to her satisfaction, he invariably picked 'Gloria in Excelsis' (but not during the grieving season of Lent, when it could not be sung, being celebratory), singing the first line a cappella, *Glory to God in the Highest, and Peace to His People on Earth*, and the choir picked up after that. It was not an idle preference on his part, but one that had a very important distinction, for these words, taken almost but not quite verbatim from the Book of Luke, were historically attributed to some time between the first and the third century.

This hymn was the one that had inspired her father as he walked in patrol one evening at the edge of a jungle next to a Vietnamese rice field, after a particularly fierce gunfight.

It was with this hymn that her father in turn fired her own inspiration. These were no ordinary words, since angels, joyfully heralding to astounded shepherds the birth of the newborn King, had uttered them. Yes, the same angels as in the mid-eighteenth-century Christmas carol 'Hark, The Herald Angels Sing', for this was no ordinary king either; it was the Son of God.

As Father Clancy read aloud three Scriptures, Tara followed along, using a little blue seasonal *Missalette*. At the conclusion of the Readings, a lay person stepped up to the podium and recited, "And we pray that our brave American and Allied troops now in harm's way in Afghanistan return safely to their homes after their duties are done."

The congregation responded, "Lord hear our prayer." Tara added her own simple thoughts silently; please take care of my daughter and my mother. She deliberately used the phrases 'my daughter' and 'my mother', so that God would have no question as to which particular Isabella and which particular Jamie. She refrained from asking for any help for

12

herself, for He had the rest of the world that needed His attention.

A group of children, belonging to the same family tree judging by their facial similarities, solemnly approached the altar, bearing in a golden bowl unleavened wheaten bread that would become the Body of Christ, and in a gold chalice diluted grape wine that would become the Blood of Christ. As the priest silently prayed over the bread and wine, the choir broke into another hymn, the Sanctus, that was also one of her favorites.

Holy, holy, holy Lord,

God of power and might,

Heaven and earth are full of Your glory.

Hosanna in the highest.

Blessed is he who comes in the name of the Lord.

Hosanna in the highest.

"Let us pray," intoned Father Clancy. They got up to sing *Pater Noster*, the Lord's Prayer, or as Jamie called it, "Song of Tears". Jamie stood on the pew, and Tara wrapped her arm around Jamie's little waist and held her close.

"Our Father who art in Heaven," recited Father Clancy, his voice booming across the church. Tara whispered under her breath, in Latin, as she remembered her father doing so, starting a full quarter of a century earlier, *Pater noster, qui es in caelis.* Then Tara would go silent, followed by thoughts that probably would never have crossed her father's mind. *Rest in peace, my Daddy, who art in Heaven.* On this cue, always, her tears began, stifled into a small handkerchief tucked away in the palm of her hand.

"Hallowed be Thy Name."

A silent *Sanctificetur nomen tuum* amidst sharp intakes of breath for lungs gasping for air.

"Thy Kingdom come,"

Adveniat regnum tuum. Only the *Ad* would come out, the rest jumbled incomprehensibly while in transit from her mind to her tongue.

"Thy Will be done,"

Fiat voluntas tua,

"On Earth,"

in terra,

"As it is in Heaven."

14

et sicut in caelo,

"Give us this day our daily bread,"

Panem nostrum quotidianum da nobis hodie.

"and forgive us our trespasses,"

Et dimitte nobis debita nostra,

"as we forgive those who trespass against us."

Sicut et nos dimittimus debitoribus nostris. God, why is it that some things in life are just so beyond forgiveness, beyond repentance, beyond redemption, beyond salvation?

"And lead us not into temptation,"

Et ne nos inducas in tentationem. But when people do succumb, thereafter remain standing no winners, only losers all around.

"but deliver us from evil."

sed libera nos a malo.

Amen.

"Deliver us, Lord, from every evil, and grant us peace in our day. In Your mercy keep us free from sin and protect us from all anxiety as we wait in joyful hope for the coming of our Savior, Jesus Christ," said Father Clancy. That

15

was all she wanted, to be free of evil, so that she could once again regain her peace. What else was there to ask? Father Clancy seemed to make it all so easy, and Tara's malaise finally started to evaporate.

Tara joined the congregation in their collective response, "For the kingdom, the power, and the glory are Yours, now and forever."

Father Clancy raised his arms. "May the peace of the Lord be always with you. I now invite you to offer each other the sign of peace."

Tara bent down and kissed Jamie on the top of her head. "Peace be with you, Jamie." And then straightening, she kissed her mother on the cheek, "And peace be with you. Ma," before shaking hands with others close by. As she reached out her hand to the lovely couple with the new baby daughter, Tara's thumb anxiously searched out where her own wedding band had once proudly nested, only to be harshly met by bare skin.

Her grip on her daughter tightened, until Jamie squirmed in pain and broke free to nestle against Isabella. Turning around, Tara blindly stuck her hand out, uttering "May peace be with you." A round-faced young girl with braces and stringy hair giggled and took her hand, while a gangly, pimply boy stood with his arm around her waist.

The priest carefully broke the consecrated bread, the Body of Christ, into pieces, as the choir then began singing *Agnus Dei*, or Lamb of God.

Lamb of God, who takes away the sins of the world,

have mercy on us.

Lamb of God, who takes away the sins of the world,

have mercy on us.

Lamb of God, who takes away the sins of the world,

have mercy on us.

Grant us peace.

The congregation knelt down in *adoration* on low, padded rests built into the pews as Father Clancy held up the consecrated Host high above his head with both hands. This was the truest core belief of Catholicism; this was not a mere reenactment of the Sacrifice of Calvary; this was an unbloodied continuation, with the consecrated bread and wine being the Body and Blood of Jesus, as He had proclaimed to His disciples at the Last Supper.

"Behold the Lamb of God, behold Him who takes away the sins of the world," before taking a small piece and placing it on his tongue. Then with both hands he lifted the chalice to his lips and took a sip of the consecrated wine, the Blood of Christ. Setting it down, he meticulously wiped the lip of the chalice with a white piece of cloth.

Then the congregation filed up to the altar to receive the Body of Christ and the Blood of Christ in Holy Communion, for in the Gospel of John, Jesus himself had stated that he who ate His flesh and drank His blood would have eternal life, and shall be raised on the Last Day.

But the Catholic church had set in place a few restrictions on who could receive Holy Communion, and although at the present time Tara was in a state of grace, she knew that it could not continue. This was at the root of Tara's sense of foreboding, for she had made an appointment to see Father Clancy after Mass, having no real choice in the matter.

All too soon, Tara realized with a sinking heart, the Mass came to an end. Finally *Ite, Missa est.* "The Lord be with you," said the priest, in dismissal, "The Mass is ended, go in peace."

༄ ༄ ༄ ༄ ༄

After Mass, they filed into the multipurpose room, where doughnuts were arranged in platters on one table, and others held coffee and tea for adults, and apple and grape juice for kids. Tara lightly held onto Jamie's shoulder and guided her through the crowd, reaching for a cup of apple juice first before helping herself to a cup of black coffee brewed in an electric pot. Isabella sidled up to her, and Tara took a quick sip before handing it to her mother. "It really tastes pretty bad, Ma."

"So why are you giving it to me?"

Caffeine is caffeine. "Would you like a jelly doughnut?" Tara glanced at the other table. "Looks like they ran out of the plain ones."

"Would you like one, dear?" someone behind the table asked Jamie, who shook her head.

"No, thank you. I'm allergic to milk, eggs, nuts and dairy," said Jamie, looking straight up at the lady.

"Oh, you are? You poor thing!"

"Good job, Jamie," said Tara, patting her on the arm approvingly. "You knew exactly what to say. And I liked how you said *No, thanks.*"

Father Clancy approached Tara, and asked softly, "I understand you wanted to discuss divorce?" In spite of having mentally rehearsed the imagined dialog in her mind, Tara was nonplussed and very embarrassed. Unlike at the Confessional, this would be done face to face, without the cover of anonymity.

Before she could reply, Tara heard Jamie's voice pipe up, clear as a bell, "My Daddy was banging my baby-sitter, so Mommy fired them both." Tara cocked her head at the priest and raised her eyebrows. Truthfully, that just about summed up the whole sordid situation.

"Very well, then. Shall we discuss this further in my office?" He looked pointedly at Jamie, and then back at Tara. "Would you like to have someone watch your daughter while we talk in private?"

Tara nodded. "My mother is here; she can do so." As they walked towards Isabella, Tara softly asked Jamie "Where did you pick up that little tidbit about the baby-sitter?"

"I heard you talking on the phone to somebody last month. That's what you said, I heard you." Jamie's brow crinkled.

"In any event, it's not nice at all to overhear other people's conversations and repeat them."

"Well, you are my Mommy! You are not other people."

"Why, thank you. But I think you know what I mean, sweetheart. Don't do it again, OK?" Leaving Jamie with Isabella, Tara hurried to Father Clancy's office.

⚘ ⚘ ⚘ ⚘ ⚘

One drizzly spring morning in 1995, Todd had wed Tara with the explicit vows *I, Todd Scott Preston, take you, Tara Rose Morgan, to be my wife, to have and to hold, from this day forward, for better or for worse, for richer or for poorer, in sickness and in health, until death do us part.* Father Clancy had been the officiating priest. He had also baptized Jamie, the fruit of their marriage. To Tara, this meeting was definitely a humiliating admission of failure.

"I found him in my marital bed with the baby-sitter, both in a very compromising position," she said with eyes downcast.

"Have you considered forgiveness," asked Father Clancy.

Tara nodded. "Of course, Father." That lie would cost about fifty Hail Marys. But the fact of the matter was that while he and the baby-sitter were upstairs going at it, violating the sanctity of her marital bed, her five-year-old daughter was downstairs coughing her head off; not a normal cough, but a barking crouping cough. That, she could not forgive.

Besides, even if she forgave him, which was something that Tara had decided to not do, he was presently living in sin with that baby-sitter, who happened to be a very attractive

21

eighteen-year-old Brazilian tramp. She was desperately in need of a green card and would do anything to get it. Tara did not want him back. It was as simple as that. "But we are now divorced."

"When did your civil divorce become final?" asked Father Clancy, lips pursed, for she had kept the proceedings private.

It was really one heck of a very uncivil divorce. "Last month." All of the papers had been signed and so on. It was all over. Nothing more to see. Just move on.

"From the position of the Church," cautioned Father Clancy, "that raises a very serious question concerning your marital status." Divorce was a civil decree granted by the state and was not recognized by the Catholic Church at all. So a divorced Catholic nevertheless remained in good standing and could continue to receive the sacraments. "Do you intend to ever remarry in the future?"

"Well, I certainly hope so, Father. I am only thirty and not quite ready to hang up my apron." Tara knew that could cause problems of a particularly difficult nature. When a Catholic man and a Catholic woman married willingly and without duress, they formed a sacramental bond that was indissoluble.

The very vows that they had exchanged attested to that belief and there was nothing in the vows that somehow included an escape clause. So even though she had legally binding documents that had indeed dissolved the marriage, as far as the Catholic Church was concerned, she was still married to the same man whom she had wedded at that very church.

If she remarried without a Declaration of Nullity, then in the eyes of the Catholic Church, she would be committing an act of adultery, placing her in a state of mortal sin. At the very least, she would be barred from receiving Holy Communion, effectively excluding her from the most precious privilege of being a Catholic.

They then started to speak about the day that she had wedded her husband, only to stop after a few minutes as her tears made it difficult to proceed. But it had to be done, as Father Clancy had to reaffirm his assessment of her mental and emotional state on that day. She confirmed that she had indeed married Todd willingly and voluntarily, which she really had, in spite of her mother's cautionary exhortations to not do so. They concluded their meeting soon afterwards.

ço ço ço ço ço

Isabella again drove the Range Rover on the way back home. "So are you going to tell me what happened back there?" she asked.

"Well, Monsignor asked me to forgive him." And take him back. And live a normal Catholic rest of their lives, devoted to each other and procreating more cute little babies. I would just as soon slit my own throat with a rusty knife before that happens, thought Tara.

"Did you ask Monsignor about petitioning the church for an Annulment?" That had been Isabella's specific directive. According to civil law in the state of New Jersey, his very act of infidelity provided the grounds for divorce. Not according to the Catholic Church, however, which only required that he go to Confession.

"Todd needs to state that he entered into marriage without a commitment." In reality, Tara herself could make the same statement, but of course then she would be lying.

Todd had no reason to make that statement anymore even though in his case it would be truthful. Although he was raised a Catholic, he was of the kind that paid a visit to the church for Christmas only, if that. Besides, the civil divorce had already been finalized. In spite of a fearsome reputation for being partial to the husbands, the judge rightly, but nevertheless unexpectedly, had taken Todd severely to task for his many unspeakable transgressions, even to the extent of stripping him of all parental rights, as Tara had explicitly requested.

She had missed the best opportunity, before the papers were signed, to force Todd to agree to the annulment. Raising the issue afterward would only have given him the upper hand, enabling him to demand visitation rights, and more. Her lawyers had very skillfully and expertly executed the legal and financial aspects of her case, but in their singleminded focus they had all overlooked the religious implications, which should have been the first item of contention, until it was too late.

"Where would an annulment leave my granddaughter?" asked Isabella. "Did you ask him that?"

Of course, she had. "He said that it has no civil bearing on the legitimacy of children. The legitimacy of any children involved is never an issue in the eyes of the Catholic Church."

Tara whipped her head around to coldly admonish Jamie, "And you are to never repeat my private conversations to anyone, got it?" But she well knew that most probably Jamie had long forgotten her blurt, and was probably clueless as to why she was being reprimanded.

Sunday Evening at the
Riverview Medical Center

2:00 p.m., Sunday, January 6, 2002. Navesink River, Middletown.

After returning from church, daughter and grandmother had stated their intentions to take the Range Rover and shop for groceries at Sickles Market, family-owned since 1908. Usually that took about an hour and a half, while they scanned the shelves for new items for Jamie to try. Isabella very carefully scrutinized each and every label, searching for ingredients to avoid, such as dairy, egg and nuts, to which Jamie was severely allergic.

Tara passed on an invitation to accompany them, since she had already made plans to pal around with her best friend, Tracey Avalon. Tracey was endowed with two rather striking attributes; one being a perfectly symmetrical and harmonious body that was simply gorgeous; the other being a propensity to spend her husband Walter's immense wealth like it was going out of style.

"I'll pick you up," Tracey had said over the phone. The car that she had ordered during the summer of 2000 had finally arrived from England; it was a handmade beauty, a fiery arrest-me red Aston Martin V8 Vantage convertible, or Roadster, as the brochure had referred to it.

Although the weekend had been an unusually cold and soggy one, even for New Jersey in January, it was nevertheless a good shopping day. Post-Christmas sales notwithstanding, the weather kept many at bay. First, they would go to a late lunch at McLoone's Riverside restaurant in Sea Bright, and then go shopping in Red Bank.

Tara was on the porch feeding the dogs when Tracey pulled up and got out of the car, saying, "Why aren't you dressed already? You heard me say that I was picking you up at three! Did you go to church dressed like that?"

"At least I went to church," said Tara. And where was she? Probably praying to St. Mattress. "It's raining, it's pouring, and it's yucky out there," she said.

Tracey's long-sleeved woolen narrow-necked jacket in rose pink swooped down to mid-thigh. The jacket was buttoned fully from the neck down to the midriff only, and flared out onto a matching pair of shorts that stopped short of the jacket's hem. A metallic silver hooded raincoat with a silver-fox trim covered her up to mid-calf, where a pair of crisscrossed python boots in rosewood and silver met it.

"Your minge is in danger of freezing shut, girlfriend," said Tara, knowing that Tracey was fully expecting to get dropped off curbside, and wanted Tara to drive.

"Never mind my minge! I'm not going out with you looking like a bush pig," said Tracey, firmly taking Tara by the arm and walking her back into the house. "Let's go get you into something that screams that the drive-thru is open."

That was one nice thing about good friends; they never hesitate to slap you in the face until good reason sets in. Their acquaintance had started at the time that Jamie was born. Tara had retained the services of a young Au Pair on a yearlong visa from England, to help her with Jamie. It so turned out that Tracey had an *Au Pair* to look after her infant son, and the two Au Pairs started to hang out with one another.

Tara's social interaction with Tracey, which had revolved around their kids' full social calendar, had never fully matured into a true friendship until much later. Over the course of the years, play dates for Tracey's clique eventually came to only mean imbibing adult drinks while the Au Pairs chatted with each other, leaving the kids to their own devices.

At times, Tara had a hunch that perhaps stronger substances than alcohol were present, and after a while, she simply had stopped going to these events. The other mothers perceived her seemingly snooty rejection of their lifestyle as a personal affront by one of their peers.

Upon her divorce from her husband of five years, many of the mothers, successful women who had placed their corporate careers on indefinite hold, viewed her with great suspicion. In their narrow, insecure minds, a divorced female, young, attractive, white and well off, was a ravenous shark in bloodied waters. Nothing would have suited them better than to see Tara run out of town on the next train out, with a big S branded on her forehead. They had met her announcement of an imminent divorce with stony hearts.

Subsequently, she had heard indirectly of a few catty questions as to why a young man would stray when he had such a lovely wife; there surely had to be something wrong with her.

It was during that time of emotional distress that Tracey had come to Tara's aid. At first, it was a shared pot of afternoon tea. Then Tracey started to withdraw from her clique, and increasingly spent more time with Tara. At more than a superficial level, they seemed like sisters, which neither of them had. Tara liked her spontaneity and Tracey liked her acquiescence, and it worked out to advancing their friendship.

Friendships had come her way only infrequently, especially after her father's demise; some of her shallower friends had dumped her instantly while others, forbidden by their parents to any further contact with her, as if her father's death by his own hands was somehow contagious and would consume them with its voracious appetite, reluctantly, shamefully and quietly receded away into the distance. In hindsight, given the especially tough turbulence of adolescence, Tara had to concede the validity of the parents' concerns.

Isabella embraced Tracey with some reservation, perceiving her friendship as a welcome breeze in Tara's life, but had made it clear that it was one that needed to be monitored for signs of leading her astray.

ভ৩ ভ৩ ভ৩ ভ৩ ভ৩

Sandwiched on a thin sliver of land between the Shrewsbury River to the west and the Atlantic Ocean to the East, Tim McLoone's restaurant, once known proudly as the Rum Runner, but since renamed to a staidly Riverside Dining, was warm inside, despite the blustery wind, rain and cold just beyond its panoramic glass windows. A short-haired woman in a tuxedo was playing a piano near the bar, taking requests from her steady fans.

Going out to lunch on Sunday worked out for both of them; Saturdays were taken up with running errands, and on Sunday mornings both attended the same church. They started off by ordering a raw platter of crab, shrimp, clams and oysters. Tara happily chose a pot of steaming Darjeeling tea, while Tracey loudly and smugly proclaimed, "I am not driving," and ordered a glass of Sauvignon Blanc. That was the other reason she wanted Tara to drive.

"How are the kids?" asked Tara. Jason was the about eight months older than Jamie, he was born in January, she in September, but they were nevertheless in the same class, since the cutoff was October. Rusty, all pimply and painfully shy at fourteen, was her son by another mother, as she spoke of him to Tara.

Tracey cracked open another crab leg. "Rusty has now taken to starching his pajamas."

That did not sound normal to Tara, and she said that it must be very uncomfortable.

Tracey pointed at Tara with her fork. "You are just having a blonde moment. Just wait until you have a teenaged boy living in your household." He was such a gusher too, added Tracey, just like his father.

"Stop!" protested Tara, shuddering at the image and laying down an uneaten oyster on the half-shell, quite nauseated. A teenaged boy living in her household was not happening, she said, especially now that she was divorced.

But, Tracey pointed out, ten years hence, what else could Jamie be bringing home, other than a skanky, pimpled boy.

"How did you find out about Rusty's starching?" asked Tara, "You don't even do the laundry!"

"The maid refused to wash his jammies and his tighty-whities anymore." First, the maid had refused to wash Walter's underwear anymore, complaining of his sloppy racing stripes down the back. Six months later came this rebellion. Tracey exclaimed that she had no idea who was doing Rusty's and Walter's laundry anymore, and that was not her problem.

"As far as I am concerned, she can haul her little self straight back to Guatemala," huffed Tracey, snapping her fingers, "Inmigración!"

"It's too cold for a glass of wine," Tracey complained to a passing waiter who mistakenly answered her summons, and accepted his recommendations of a hot Toddy. "Oops,

32

sorry!" she said to Tara, whose ex-husband was Todd Scott Preston, nicknamed Toddy. "If that pianist so much as starts on the Piano Man song we are leaving."

"I doubt it," Tara said, noting that the lady was belting out pretty decent renditions of British tavern songs.

"Rusty's also been going through my Vanity Fair," said Tracey. "I had to fight him for the latest today just so that I could take it to church with me. He's dog-eared all the interesting pages, and that makes it look like I have a dirty mind." Never mind what she was doing taking such a scandalous magazine to church, she huffed.

Maybe she should just get him his own subscription as a coming-of-age present, Tara suggested. Tracey waved her hand dismissively, "Why should I have to pay for his dirty habits?" He could continue to intercept her Vickie's Secret catalogs, if he could pry them from Walter's hands, she scoffed.

The Aston Martin had not come purely out of the good-ness and magnanimity of Walter's heart, as Tara knew. A particular transgression that had forced its purchase was Walter's secret fondness for Internet porn. Tracey had come across it the old-fashioned way, by snooping, even though his computer was protected by a password; the fool had merely penciled it on the flip side of his mouse pad, and there was really no reason whatsoever to do so, since it was just his middle name, Daniel. Walter manned up to the transgression, obviously with copious embarrassment, and had not tried to blame it on his son.

"So," said Tracey, smiling brightly, "that's what I have been doing. How about you?"

Tara told her about that morning's conversation with the Monsignor, putting on an air of nonchalance, not wanting to burden her friend with matters that had no easy resolution.

"Don't take those banal platitudes to heart for even one moment! What didn't you get, sister? That's just their way of saying that five grand will get you an annulment pretty pronto, no nosy questions asked," said Tracey, snapping her fingers in an annoying rapid-fire. "Just write out the check and be done with it!"

Tara shook her head. That would be living a lie. After all, she had Jamie as living proof of that the marriage had taken place sacramentally as well as legally. Basically, in her mind Todd had brought shame and indignity on her, and she had to live with the consequences while he went happily on his way continuing to spill his seed into the hussy.

If Tara had just pulled out a Smith & Wesson and shot that philanderer – bang, bang – right between his cheating eyes, all that she would have had to do was beg forgiveness, and the church would have granted her exactly that. Go figure, she thought.

"I thought that I had a life companion," she said, now realizing that she was sadly mistaken.

"Are you going back to work?" Tracey asked, for Tara had been working as an investment banker at the tony firm of Goldman, Sachs at the southernmost tip of Lower Manhattan until that dreadful morning of September 11 of 2001, when she had seen the Twin Towers fall.

She had no need to work, but in addition to money, she had inherited her mother's work ethic, which meant that she had to keep herself employed. Also, the distraction of a full-time job could be a salve to her scars, not all of which were mental. But the combination of failed global policies, 9/11, the dot-com bust in Silicon Valley and finally the telecom meltdown of 2001 had seemingly tolled the end of the American Century. Investment money had dried up, and even strong companies were slashing their payrolls to the bone by laying people off, or by shipping white- and blue-collar jobs alike overseas to India or China.

Tara replied that she did not have a clear idea about what she would be doing, but it had to be local, preferably in Red Bank.

"I have never seen you so down," said Tracey, her face dark.

"Oh, I'm not despondent," said Tara, thankful of her friend's concern. After all, these were the cards that had been dealt to her, and she had little choice to play them to the best of her abilities. Unlike the old song by Kenny Rogers, often one did not have the option of folding and walking or running away. She was just thirty years old, and had the best years of her lifetime ahead of her.

Tracey set aside her fork. "I got to admire your spunk," she said, "If I had been in your sorry shoes I would surely have downed the old hemlock." Tracey was not being insensitive; she was merely ignorant of her father's suicide.

☙ ☙ ☙ ☙ ☙

Tara carefully licked off the whipped cream and foamy milk of her cappuccino with the tip of her tongue, much to the obvious delight of a set of very dreamy early twenty-something twins with long blonde hair swept back, eating at the bar, in cargo pants, hooded designer sweatshirts and unlaced virgin work boots that never saw a construction site. The peach fuzz hair on their chins and arms was also a golden blonde, highlighting their tanned skins, probably fresh from Christmassing somewhere very warm. She caught their appreciative looks, and smiled at them out of self-consciousness. Just a *hello, nice to see you too* kind of smile, nothing more.

Tracey caught her little maneuver and whispered, "You go, girl!"

They split the tab, as was their routine, and donned their coats. Tara led the way as they walked past the bar on their way out. The afternoon crowd had started to pour in, and as Tara glanced over her shoulder to make sure that Tracey was right behind her, she felt a hand catch her in the small of her back and push her hard to the left. She in turn jostled the arm of one of the twins, spilling most of his drink.

"I'm so terribly sorry," she said, reaching out to touch his shoulder while turning around to scowl at the perpetrator, Tracey. She did not stop, but deliberately kept on walking towards the exit.

Once they were in the car and underway, Tracey said, "I can't believe that you screwed up on a great opportunity to buy those twofers a drink."

"So why didn't *you* jump on that opportunity," asked Tara. Those were still just kids! "Did you see the look on their faces," said Tara a moment later, smiling. "They almost fell over. The next time, make sure to card them first. But seriously, what do I do, Trace?"

"Girlfriend, you need a booty call," said Tracey. "I was merely trying to help, but there was nobody home when I tried putting that call through. Thank you for using AT&T. Is there anything else that we can help you with? Your bag is beeping," said Tracey, opening it with no hesitation and retrieving Tara's cell phone.

A missed phone call from her mother had gone straight to voice-mail. *Hi. We were on our way home, but Jamie has a swollen lip. It looks like a large blister on her entire lower lip. I'll call you back in a few minutes if I don't hear from you. Bye.*

Tara felt the hair on the back of her neck stand. She hit the speed-dial on the phone, and Isabella answered the phone immediately. "Tara, her lower lip's blown up like an inner tube." She had just dispensed two chewable tablets of Children's Benadryl to Jamie. They had just passed the Red Bank Post Office on Broad Street, and were now stopped at the light in front of the Jade Garden Chinese restaurant.

"Ma! Go straight to the emergency room at Riverview and tell them that she is having an allergic reaction. Right now!

Got that? We are just leaving McLoone's, and we will meet you there. You can pull in and just leave the truck in front of the ER. I'll be there in about ten minutes."

"You heard," Tara said to Tracey, and making an illegal U-turn, stepped on the throttle.

"Don't take River Road," Tracey cautioned, even though it was the shortest route to the Riverview Medical Center, since that would take them through the denser sections of Rumson, Fair Haven and Red Bank. Instead, Tara took the lightly traveled Ridge Road, which ran parallel to River Road. The lights were in her favor, and she made good time all the way where it merged with Harding Road, and continued for half a mile before making a right onto Broad Street.

She wondered what had caused Jamie's reaction; she had either ingested something that contained a food that she could not eat, such as milk, eggs or nuts, or she had come into contact with some such thing and then maybe touched her lips. That was why she always had Benadryl tablets with her in a little red pouch that always was with her, as was a medical alert bracelet. In the event of an ana-phylactic reaction, which could cause her entire body to fatally shut down, she also carried an Epi-Pen, which was an auto-injector that administered a life-saving dose of epinephrine, which would temporarily reverse the allergic reaction. Isabella certainly knew how to use it, and so did Jamie herself.

Tara was worried, but not as much as she would have been if her mother were not with Jamie. Isabella had a very firm personality, and was good at solving problems, having dealt with many unique hurdles.

Jamie's allergies had become evident at an early age. At four months, Tara had spooned her a tiny amount of plain whole yogurt sweetened with pureed peaches. Within seconds, huge welts had appeared, doubling her lips in size. Tara had immediately recognized the symptoms, having had a childhood friend who was severely allergic to peanuts. She had administered liquid Benadryl, and then had called 911.

Tara spotted the Range Rover parked erratically in front of the eatery whimsically named *Flaky Tart*, and she slammed on the brakes, pulling right behind the truck, in the handicapped zone. She got out of the Aston Martin and ran to the truck; it was unlocked, and she opened the rear passenger door.

No one was inside, but the stench was overpowering, and Tara instinctively stepped back. There was vomit all over the back of the driver's seat, and on Jamie's booster seat.

Just before slamming the door shut, Tara noticed large yellow chunks that looked like bits of foam. Horrible as the scene was, Tara was glad that Jamie had thrown up, which meant that the offending allergens were not still inside her body, continuing to causing more havoc.

Tracey's face was ashen, but she had the presence of mind to ask a couple of teenage Hispanic girls who were nearby, "Do you know where they are," pointing to the Range Rover.

"Si, policía los tomó," came the reply, and a couple of hands pointed north.

"¿Fueron ellos al hospital," asked Tara, hoping that her high-school Spanish was still passable, to which they nodded. "¿Fue ella bien," she asked, to which they shrugged their shoulders, faces expressing concern.

"Drive!" Tara yelled to Tracey, resisting the urge to heave, and hitting Send on her cell phone, but the calls did not go through due to dead-zones. It only took a couple of minutes for them to pull up at the entrance to the emergency room, right behind a Red Bank police cruiser, which was empty too, its lights still eerily flashing.

Leaving Tracey to park the car, Tara ran inside, her eyes frantically looking around, but could not see Jamie or Isabella. "Excuse me," she said, cutting in front of an elderly couple waiting in line, "my daughter, Jamie Morgan? Has she been admitted yet?"

"Just a moment, please," came the reply, as the couple waved her on. "I'm sorry, but I do not see anyone by that name. Let me try it again, M-O-R-G-A-N. Are you sure she was brought here?"

"Try Jamie Preston." The old copy of Jamie's medical insurance card that was in Isabella's purse probably still read Preston; the replacement one that she herself had stated Morgan. Then the receptionist asked for Tara's identification. The name Tara Rose Morgan on the driver's license did not cut it as far as the receptionist was concerned, and demanded to see some form of ID such as a credit card, checkbook, student ID, anything indicating that her last name was 'Preston'.

Naturally, after the divorce, Tara had every instance of her married name reverted back to her maiden name.

Just as she started to panic, Tracey firmly grabbed her by the arm and escorted her out of the building. "Follow me, and let me do the talking," she said, and walked towards the ambulance entrance. Skirting past the old, dried pools of multihued engine oil and radiator fluid, they strode purposefully through the automatic sliding doors and into the main ER area, unchallenged. "Stay right here," Tracey commanded, and approached the nurse's station. After a quick, muted chat, she came back, pointing to one of the triage rooms.

Cautiously opening the door, Tara saw Jamie sitting up on the bed, with the police officer next to her. Isabella had the phone at her ear, looking angry. "I've been trying to get through to you for the past half an hour!" Tara was busy hugging Jamie, and did not say anything.

The officer turned to her and said, "She's doing OK. The nurse went to get the doctor. It seems that little Jamie here had a reaction." Isabella had pulled him over and with her approval he had given Jamie the shot of Epinephrine from the glove box of the Range Rover.

Jamie's drenched coat was in a plastic bag in the corner, cinched up. Tara could see the wet areas showing through the white plastic. Grabbing a handful of paper towels, she wet them in warm water and wiped the remaining dried crud off Jamie's hands, her knees and upper thighs, where her mother had missed a few spots.

"I puked," said Jamie. Tara nodded, her knees knocking, feeling very relieved and tired at the same time, mindful that this was the first time that Jamie had experienced an anaphylactic reaction, and during its apex had walked briefly in the shadows of the valley of death, and lived. In a way, the multiple levels of remedial procedures that had been indoctrinated into Tara, Isabella and Jamie had worked, at least this time; but would it work as well the next time? The two held on tight to each other.

After a polite knock on the door, a young Indian ER physician came in with a nurse, and introduced himself as Dr. Ramgopal. Tracey and the police officer excused themselves and left the room, as it was by now quite crowded.

Dr. Ramgopal examined Jamie at length before announcing that she had recovered fully, but that they would keep an eye on her for another hour or so, cautioning that she would probably be very hyper until the medicines wore off. He took down the names of Jamie's pediatrician, as well as of her allergist, and promised to send them both a detailed report. "We have been seeing quite a few such cases," he said, and commended Tara for making sure that there was always an Epi-Pen with Jamie.

Tracey was outside the triage room, chatting easily with the policeman. "He has access to their secret stash of coffee," said Tracey, holding up her paper cup for Tara.

Tara reached out to shake his hand. "Thanks a lot, Officer..." She scanned his badge. "Officer Roland. Thanks for saving my daughter's life!" He was young, she noticed, probably in his mid twenties, and had the solid, athletic build of someone who worked out regularly, with steely blue eyes and cropped brown hair. His grip was firm and warm.

Red Bank Police Officer Toby Roland raised his right hand to his right eyebrow. "Looks as though your daughter is in good hands. I will get back to my patrol. Take care."

Tracey gave her a quick hug. "Never a dull moment with kids, is there?"

භ භ භ භ භ

By the time they walked out of the hospital over an hour later, the rain had turned into a light snow. Tara was glad that Tracey had stayed, since the Range Rover still had the messy vomit in the back, rendering Jamie's seat unusable. Jamie went with Tracey in the two-seater Aston Martin while Tara and Isabella collected the Range Rover and drove it home with the windows rolled down and the fan turned up all the way to dispel the stench.

Once home, Tara prepared a cool drink to quench Jamie's thirst. Right on the counter next to the refrigerator was the aluminum pan of store-bought pound cake that Tara had taken out, and forgotten to put away. Chunks had been

45

gouged away with a spoon that was still stuck in it. Tara picked up the lid and read the ingredients; equal amounts each of flour, butter, eggs and sugar, in true tradition.

"She has never done that before," said Isabella.

Tara knew what had happened; they had recently discovered a particular yellow cake mix, free of milk powder, that Tara used to bake a passable cake without eggs or dairy, using soy milk and egg substitute instead; and they baked it in a rectangular aluminum pan.

Jamie had mistaken the pound cake for hers. Mystery solved.

Topic of Cancer

5:00 p.m., Monday, January 7, 2002. Navesink River, Middletown.

The full significance of Jamie's episode had finally hit Tara on Monday morning, after she had taken Jamie to see the allergist. Subsequently, she had moped around the house, despondent and listless, until her mother chased her out that afternoon at four to go for a drive to clear her head.

"You need some time off by yourself," was all that Isabella had said, but Tara knew to interpret that as time to perform specific introspection, and not as unfettered time.

The doctors had always warned Tara that Jamie might never grow out of her allergies. Even after over four years of dealing with the allergies, every single day, around the clock, Tara had in fact grown not complacent, but rather full of hope that Jamie had started to turn the corner.

It rankled Tara that it was not the hand of a stranger or an errant baby-sitter that had caused their first near-fatal food accident, but her own. Isabella had not given her a well-deserved censure yet about leaving the pound cake on the counter, but Tara was sure that it was on its way.

Tara drove the Porsche 911 to Red Bank's new town hall, at the corner of Maple Avenue and Monmouth Street, which housed the police station. The first, fluffy snowflakes of the day were just beginning to fall, and melted instantly into huge starbursts.

She had picked up a big bouquet of flowers that she wanted to present to the police officer who had rushed Jamie to the Riverview Medical Center. She could have merely had the florist deliver them with a *Thank you* note, but somehow that had seemed too impersonal, considering that his swift-ness had saved Jamie.

She pulled into the paved courtyard of the town hall and to avoid being an easy mark, made doubly sure that she had parked correctly in an unreserved spot, and that the car was well within the white markers. There were no parking me-ters within sight, but she made sure to check with a couple of officers taking a break, with coffee and cigarettes in their hands, huddled against the arctic gusts.

The wind howled through the automatic doors, threaten-ing to strip the petals off the flowers as she walked into the lobby of the building.

A muscular, young police officer on duty at the desk nodded warmly at her and looked at his watch. "Toby Roland? You just missed him by a few minutes." Then he turned to a grim older woman in uniform filing papers. "Didn't he say that he was going down to the marina?"

"Yeah, I think that's what he said," the woman agreed reluctantly, giving Tara a knowing look of disapproval that made her feel uncomfortable. Perhaps it was the outfit that she was wearing, thought Tara, expecting the vice squad to jump over the counter at any moment and wrestle her to the ground; calf-height embossed western boots, horizontally striped leggings, a distressed brown couture cotton mini-skirt, a matching tight jacket designed to never have the buttons meet, and a white full-sleeved turtleneck. A three-quarters length hooded Shearling coat kept her warm.

The young officer came over, hitching up his crisply creased trousers. "If you drive down Front Street you will probably catch him," he said, pointing with the sharp end of a pencil, his eyes riveted on the flowers. "Are they for him?"

Much to his credit, Tara did not detect even a hint of a leer, but still she was starting to regret bringing them. Maybe a simple note dropped in the mail would have been a smarter idea. But it was too late now. Besides, were all of the Red Bank police officers so good looking?

"Yes. He saved my daughter's life yesterday." She knew that there was no need to explain to the policeman, but her new status as a single woman made her very conscious of her words and actions.

She hastily excused herself and walked out into the parking lot, feeling ridiculous. Resisting the strong urge to just pitch the flowers and go home, she got into her Porsche and turned north onto Maple, squinting through the beads of water on the windows, searching for him.

Red bank was a pedestrian town at heart, but the stores did not have any awnings to offer any shelter. She mostly saw people ducking into some of the local restaurants and bars, and hoped that he was not among them.

At the next light, she made a quick right onto Front Street and headed east along the south bank of the Navesink River. Then, to her immense relief, she spotted him in his navy-blue regulation trench coat, under a huge black umbrella, walking alone past the Elks Club.

She was sure that there was probably a local ordinance against honking the horn, since they were only a couple of blocks away from the Riverview hospital. Pulling over next to a line of parked cars, Tara rolled down her window and shouted, "Officer Roland! Wait!"

She waved as he turned around. "Officer Roland? Remember me from yesterday?" Of course he would remember, wouldn't he?

Without any hesitation, Toby Roland smiled back at her in obvious recognition. Holding his hand up to caution the traffic, he crossed the street and came over to stand next to the Porsche. She apologized as the windshield wipers doused him with water, and turned them off. He held his umbrella over the window to keep the snowflakes off her. Cars swerved wide to avoid them, their drivers casting gleeful looks at her, surely thinking that she had been pulled over for a traffic violation.

Then she noticed the carton of pizza in his hand. "Do you deliver too?" *Nice going, Tara!* "Jamie and I got these flowers for you. Carrying the pizza and the flowers may be a bit of a handful. Let me give you a ride, please."

Toby protested at first, not wanting to drip all over the luxurious leather and wool carpet inside her car. She dismissed his objections, pointing out that she had a truck with puke all over the back seat, which had not been cleaned yet. He walked around and had difficulty getting into the car, being very tall, until she showed him how to move the seat back.

"These are very beautiful flowers. You really didn't have to do that!"

She took the wet umbrella from him and tossed it onto the tiny floor behind them. Taking advantage of a lull in the traffic, she eased back into the lane and continued east.

He pointed to a decrepit, roughly paved alleyway that ran between two low buildings. She took it slowly to avoid scraping the bottom of the sports car on the high spots. It descended steeply towards the waterfront, and she was thankful for the roughness of the fractured concrete top, which offered a lot of traction to the wide tires. The burble of the twin exhausts reverberated off the exposed, antique brick walls. Then at his direction, she made a left into the fenced repair yard of the Irwin Marina.

She had spent most of her life in the area, yet had never ventured down that particular alley. Unlike sports cars, powerboats had never caught her fancy, although they looked very pretty moored at the marina.

"Please do join me in a slice or two?" he said. "I have some Stewart's root beer in the fridge."

Tara looked at her watch. That did sound like a nice thing to do, she thought, and the melted cheese on the pizza pie smelt heavenly. Anyway, who could pass up on Stewart's root beer, traditionally a native treat of the Jersey Shore? She agreed to his offer, but only after first calling home to check up on Jamie.

Her inner voice cautioned her against divulging too much to her mother, and so she merely stated that she was not going to be home for a while, and advised them to go ahead and have their dinner.

"You can park the car anywhere," said Toby. The yard was closed to all but the owners of the boats that were moored there. "I guarantee that you will not get a parking ticket today."

"I better not get one," exclaimed Tara, pulling up close to a row of brand new pleasure boats still on their wooden palettes, tightly shrink-wrapped in white plastic, stacked three high on special steel structures accessible only by special forklift trucks. "You have no idea. This car is such a ticket magnet."

"We call the crime 'DWR', driving while rich," he said, with irony.

He carried the pizza, and she the flowers, as they walked, not quite sheltered underneath his umbrella. The narrow, glistening wooden pier extended north about hundred and fifty feet into the icy waters of the perfect natural harbor, a mile across, formed by the Navesink River as it flowed along its eight mile journey to join the Shrewsbury River, and thence to the Atlantic Ocean.

To the west was the stately Molly Pitcher Inn, and to its north lay the Oyster Point Hotel, and beyond that the newly built Cooper's Bridge. To their east lay the Riverview Medical Center, just beyond the Monmouth Sailing Club. Her own house was on the other side of the river, about a mile further east.

His boat, aptly named *Frozen Assets*, was the last one out on the pier. About a dozen motorboats ranging in length from twenty-five to thirty-five feet were berthed off smaller branches of the pier, each crosstied to the dock to prevent them from bumping into the pilings, especially on stormy days.

The only color around was that of the boats, the waters were as gray as the skies, and the snowflakes added light dabs of white onto a hauntingly beautiful panorama.

The only noise was that of nature, the water lapping fiercely at the hulls and at the dock, the wind whistling past riggings and drumming upon weathered canvas, and the subdued honks of a brood of ducks that had claimed the marina as their yearlong home, their mottled brown plumage blending into the old wood of the wharf.

That part of the marina was visible from every point on the shore, forming the watery stage of a great natural amphitheater, and yet it seemed desolate, with the only visible signs of humanity coming from the distant stream of cars silently forging their way slowly along Front Street.

If she had been with anyone else, Tara would have quickly retreated with great prudence, but she felt very safe with Toby; in the worst of circumstances, the policeman at the station knew that she was going to see Toby, and her last phone call was from the marina, and could be traced.

There was a tiny can of aerosol pepper spray on the key chain with her car keys, and also she had a sharp pocketknife in her purse. Lastly, she had undergone half a decade of training in karate as a child, and still remembered the basic moves.

She had at one time considered applying for a permit for a handgun, but Isabella had admonished her in no uncertain terms to never have one, especially since Tara's late father had shot himself with a handgun.

She took the pizza from Toby as he knelt down on the wharf and tugged on the tie-downs to pull the boat closer. It was not a floating dock, and judging by the dark watermarks on the pilings, it was a long way to high tide.

His boat appeared to be somewhat old, but seaworthy, with everything seeming to be in its place. It was, even to her untrained eyes, not originally a pleasure craft but an older coastal work boat, even perhaps formerly a small Coast Guard patrol boat. Most of its lines were straight, with the exception of the gentle swoop of the hull.

A natural canvas top covered the otherwise open flying deck, with other canvas panels protecting the instruments. The windows on the cabin were dark, and an air conditioner protruded out towards the back deck. Judging by the clean transom, it was powered by inboard engines.

Just as she began to wonder how on earth he would board the vessel, he catapulted over the wooden gunwales by holding on to brass handrails next to the coaming, and landed evenly on his feet, no doubt cushioned by his thick rubber soles.

"You are sorely mistaken if you are expecting me to pull off that monkey-boy swing," she said. "Don't you have a gangway onboard, or at the very least a ladder?" Tara asked him, with deep misgivings. To her dismay, he shook his head, saying that she would only impale herself on such a ladder, with the way the boat was heaving in the rough water. From the other side of the boat he dragged over a large, white plastic ice chest.

Let's get this circus on the road, she thought, and tossed him the pizza, which bounced off his hand and fortunately landed not into the water, but on the deck. Her handbag and then the flowers followed suit. He pointed out the wooden planks nailed horizontally to the pilings, and he commanded her to step no lower than the first one, while he hunkered down and tugged on the guy ropes to steady the boat.

She knew not to focus on the yawning chasm between the boat and the dock, but instead kept her eyes on the handrails. She grabbed them as he had done, and when he shouted *Now*, Tara swung one foot onto the gunwale, and felt the surge of adrenalin as she was lifted up effortlessly.

His powerful hand grabbed her arm and thus steadied, she managed to step gracefully on to the ice chest, and then onto the deck. How was she going to get back onto shore, she wondered, as she retrieved her handbag.

Holding the entry door open, he ushered Tara into the unexpected warmth of the dark cabin, awkwardly reaching past her to switch on the interior lights. The boat ran off dock power while it was moored. Tara looked around at the inside of the main cabin, which like the exterior of the boat was evidently of ample age, and Spartan, but very tidy.

The floor had brown carpet, and the walls were paneled with a speckled, beige laminate. A large table, attached to the hull on one side, had a top of the same laminate as the walls, with ribbed aluminum edging. The padding on the bench seating on both sides was covered in a pastel green vinyl.

It reminded her of an old, comfortable, inviting diner like the Broadway Diner on Monmouth Street, but without the garish neon signs. Turning around, she caught him giving her the once-over, but he responded with a disarming smile. She apologized for not getting a vase.

Water, water everywhere, but none for the flowers, he joked. "Here, please do off take your coat, sit down, stay a while," said Toby while he rummaged through the galley, and came up with a huge beer stein. "Guess I won't be drinking beer tonight."

"Guess not," said Tara, handing him her Shearling coat, and tugged at her skirt, which revealed about two inches of bare skin above her leggings that came up to mid-thigh. The fragrant smell of the sausage, peppers and onions reminded her that she had not eaten anything for over six hours.

"I can even pretend to be domestic and set the table for you." He took her up on that offer, showing her the galley.

Leaving her there, he retreated into the sleeping quarters, to change out of his uniform into civvies.

It would be too much to expect to find a pair of kitchen shears, she thought, and she did not want to go through all the drawers searching for one, so she used a well-used serrated steak knife to trim the stems of as many of the flowers as she could fit in the beer stein. However, she did have to open a couple of cabinets before finding dinner plates.

She then took the arrangement and placed it in the center of the table. As he had promised, there were a few bottles of Stewart's root beer, and she took two of them with her back to the table. There was a slight draft from the large window that looked out onto the marina, but there was ample heat that emanated from a built-in radiator under the table.

She heard a cell phone ring somewhere, and she checked to make sure that it was not the one in her bag. A few minutes later, it rang again, and went unanswered again.

Toby came back in, apologizing for having kept her waiting. He had changed into a pair of blue jeans and a navy sweater.

Tara flashed him a quick smile and laid out two slices, a large one for him and a smaller one for herself, while he popped the caps of the beverages with a Swiss Army knife. His fingernails were well trimmed and clean, she noticed as he handed her a bottle.

He looked to be about twenty-five, she thought, with close-cropped blonde hair and hazel eyes. His complexion was the usual winter pale, with cheeks ruddy, probably from spending a lot of time outdoors.

"I could try to button up my jacket, or I could tuck a napkin so that I don't drip all over my white blouse," Tara said, licking the oil from the melted cheese off her fingers.

"No, wouldn't want you to drip all over your white blouse. And there is positively no way that you will be able to button that jacket," noted Toby, picking up a paper napkin. "My hands are still clean. Do you want me to tuck the napkin in for you?"

Tara lifted her chin up, and patted the napkin down after he tucked it into the top of her high-necked blouse. "Now you can drip to your heart's content," he said.

She sat there for a few seconds, just surveying her meal. She could not get over how she was calmly sitting down to have dinner with a stranger, especially in his own abode. Did his profession have anything to do with her ease? After all, he had saved Jamie's life. Every second counted, and she still could not get over how close a call it had been.

Being conscious of what she ate, the pizza was a very special treat for her, and her mouth was watering at the heady aroma that so wildly exceeded that of its simple constituents: yeast, wheat, tomato, milk and shredded cow parts. They had to add some secret additive to make it so irresistible and downright addictive, she thought.

The first bite made her taste buds explode in exquisite overload; it was full of flavor, due especially to the mix of mozzarella and creamy ricotta cheese that was favored by the pizzerias of the Jersey Shore.

The thin crust, a study in contrasts, was pliable yet perfectly crunchy on the bottom, and soft and chewy on the top, but still cooked all the way through, without a doughy texture. The sausage was juicy, and the peppers and onions were still slightly crunchy. It was from Danny's Pizza on Monmouth Street.

She motioned towards a large curved sword mounted on a bulkhead. "Isn't that a Marine sword?" Aside from that, there was very little else in the way of private mementoes such as photographs, certificates, or even just the normal everyday clutter. She did know that stuff lying around on a boat would get tossed around, and everything had to be secured, but his boat could easily withstand a military inspection.

"Yes, it is! That's a genuine US Marine NCO sword, and you are looking at a genuine former Marine," he said, with an appreciative nod. "I am impressed that you recognized it. Let me guess? Someone in your family was in the Marines; husband, father, or brother? Or a collector of things military?"

She knew why he had to use the word husband, and decided to not fall for that trap. "My father served as a Marine in Vietnam. I have his sword at home, but it seems a bit different than yours."

She knew the distinction between ex-Marine and former Marine. Her father had made that quite abundantly clear *Once a Marine, always a Marine.* A Marine who had retired or left the service with honor was always referred to as a former Marine; someone who got thrown out of the service with dishonor was an ex-Marine

"That is the oldest weapon still used in any service. It is the old Cavalry Sword," he said. "If your father's is different, then his is the Mameluke, which tells me he was an officer."

He had started off as a Second Lieutenant, and left the war as a Captain. She did not tell him that he did get wounded, but not as a result of enemy fire; somehow he had accidentally shot himself in the butt. Her father never really talked about it, but she knew that one of his buddies had to hoist him onto his shoulders and wade through miles of rice fields to get him to a Huey helicopter. Back at the base, they had stitched him up in a hurry and threw him right back. Of course, one does not receive a Purple Heart for self-inflicted wounds, however accidental.

"When were you in the Marines?" she asked Toby.

He had been dispatched to Okinawa, until a year ago when he was discharged for medical reasons. And then he came back and found a nice job with the Red Bank police.

It was nice that he got to go overseas, she thought, especially in peacetime, and to Japan. But what sort of medical reasons, she wondered to herself, having read on the Internet about the wild sex trades that were rampant around the military bases there.

"How's your daughter doing?" he asked, obviously changing the subject. "Will she ever outgrow her food allergies?"

Jamie was back to her normal self since waking up that morning, she said, thanking him for asking. It was possible, she said, that Jamie would outgrow them, but only time would tell.

Two slices of pizza each was all that they needed to be satiated. Dinner finished, Tara got up and took both plates to the sink and washed her hands before retrieving her coat.

"Thanks for dinner. Call me sometime," offered Tara. "Do you have a pen?"

Toby started rummaging for one. Tara opened her bag, took out her lipstick and scribbled her cell phone number with it on a clean paper napkin. "Here. Please do call," she said, handing it to him. He received it with both hands, in the Japanese way, a warm smile of satisfaction spreading on his face.

As she turned away and walked out onto the back of the boat, Tara thought she heard Toby say "*Brrrrrngg, brrrrngggg. Brrrrrngg, brrrrngggg.*" She stopped in her tracks, turned around and saw him holding his thumb to his ear, and his pinky reaching to his lips, with an impish smile.

"Hi, it's me Toby." He wanted to know what she was going to be doing on Valentine's Day. It was over a month away, she thought to herself, why would he not have asked for a date sooner? Not that it really mattered, since she had no desire to go out on a date just yet with anyone, but was there a girlfriend in the wings? She did not see anything inside the cabin that even remotely hinted of a feminine touch.

She replied that she had plans with her family, again avoiding mentioning a significant other, but recognizing that by omission, she had signaled that she had none.

"What about the evening before?"

She had to admit that usually not many would have had the nerve to continue; but as a policeman and a Marine, surely he had to always be self-confident in order to even survive.

"What about it?"

"Want to go out with me, Tara?"

Tara sighed deeply. "I really am not looking for a relationship, Toby." It had nothing to do with him. She had not been out on a date, other than with her ex-husband, in over seven years. That was in spite of Tracey's exhortations to go find a younger boy toy.

"Well, that's just peachy-keen-dandy-perfect! Neither am I." He suggested a nice sushi dinner.

She wrinkled her nose. "Hard to get really fresh great sushi around here."

"I do know of a particular place that specializes in really fresh great sushi."

"I don't know. Well, if you really insist. What time will you pick me up?" They were still talking into their 'pretend' phones.

"Ah, that's a slight problem; I don't have a personal car. I got the regulation, standard issue Crown Vic with the light bar, and I have a motorbike."

She needed to make sure that she had the story straight. Here he was, asking her out to a – what was it – really fresh great sushi dinner, but he had no wheels. Did she miss anything? Because it felt like when she first got her driver's license, and had to play bus driver to every other brat who had no wheels. Tara shook her head.

"Whatever. Sure. Oh, by the way, why aren't you looking for a serious relationship?" Wasn't she pretty 'nuff for him? Or was he really a gay boy looking for a female cover? Tara playfully leaned over to push down one of her leggings.

"I have terminal cancer."

Tara dropped her 'pretend' phone. "That's not funny at all, Toby!" she rebuked him, quite angrily.

"Well, hell yes! It would be deliriously funny if it weren't the truth, the whole truth and nothing but the truth."

"Oh my God. I'm sorry. Oh my God!" Tara felt her cheeks flush with embarrassment.

He shrugged. "Not your fault. You had nothing to do with it. Anyway, it's no big deal, really. Besides, I don't want you to get all upset and cancel our dinner."

Tara shook her head. "I won't. I promise. I am not quite as shallow as I may appear to you."

"You would be surprised how many are." His blue eyes were very sincere.

"So why did you take a chance and tell me?"

"You have a kid with a serious life-threatening medical problem. I gambled that you would understand." Toby said.

Just how 'terminal' was his cancer, she wondered, rubbing the back of her neck, which was now beginning to throb with the stress.

Two years ago the VA doctors had given him one year, if even that. Apparently, they had been quite wrong about that, because here he was, standing in front of her, still tickin'." But basically, his cancer had metastasized; he was living on borrowed time.

She watched in disbelief as Toby reached into his pockets and pulled out a brand new pack of cigarettes. Tapping one out, he stuck it nonchalantly in the corner of his mouth and cupped his hands around a lighter. A characteristic puff of pale blue smoke rose in front of him, which he swatted away with a dismissive wave of his hand. He had terminal cancer, and he still smoked?

He stood with his legs apart, his back straight, his head level, looking straight into her eyes. "A condemned man is entitled to a cigarette," he said, taking a long drag on it. "What? I should now be worried about dying of lung cancer? The funny thing is that even if I got lung cancer today, I still would live longer than with the type I have!"

It was hard to debate that point, she conceded. "I still don't want a serious relationship. You understand that, right?"

"Absolutely Roger that," he said with a flip salute. "I wouldn't want a sympathy date anyway."

Good, she thought, she would never give sympathy dates anyway. The realization that she did have a vague idea of what he was seeking, and that at some selfish level it may have had some appeal to her, definitely bothered her. In reality, given Jamie's condition, the last thing that she needed was another very sick person to worry about. "I have to leave now," she said. "Good night, Toby."

In the Company of Middle-aged White Men

8:00 a.m., Tuesday, January 15, 2002. Red Bank.

Tara Morgan parked the Porsche on Broad Street in front of the Flaky Tart Cafe. She quietly headed toward the back of the restaurant, where five minutes later a young waitress brought her a hefty cup of steaming cappuccino and a raspberry scone with orange marmalade and a pat of whipped butter.

At five minutes to eight, Tara reluctantly pushed the remnants of her cappuccino away and walked out onto Broad Street.

Two blocks later, she stopped at a magnificent century-old stone building, and paused briefly to read the brightly polished brass sign with blackened lettering:

Trundle, Morgan & Dickey, LLP

Investment Banking

Red Bank, New Jersey

Her jaw clenched tightly, Tara entered the lobby of the firm that her father had founded.

"Hello, may I help you?" A young woman in a faux leopard-skin coat chimed up, flashing two rows of pearly white Chiclets teeth.

"Yes, thank you. I'm Tara Morgan. I believe that Mr. Jack Mulholland is expecting me."

"Of course! Please do sit down, and I will inform Mr. Mulholland that you are here," said the receptionist with a bright smile. Tara sat down in a large, classic Corbusier chrome and black leather club chair. 8.15 am. Her appointment was to have started at 8 am.

Beyond the receptionist, Tara spotted the two elevators, both with doors of polished brass.

It was noon on that infamous Monday of October 19 1987, which came to be darkly known as Black Monday. Tara, as always, had rushed from the cloistered compound of Red Bank Catholic High School to meet her father in that very lobby for a quick lunch. This time, she had waited almost ten minutes for him. When he did come, he had rushed out of the elevator on the left, the sleeves of his blue starched cotton shirt folded halfway up his arms, and the collar unbuttoned. He had appeared quite cross.

"Where were you?" he had demanded to know. "I've been calling the school looking for you!"

"I was in the bathroom, Daddy," she had lied.

"We can talk about that later," he had said, cutting her short. "Unfortunately I cannot have lunch with you today."

"Why, what's the matter, Daddy?"

"The stock market went into a tailspin. It's been free-falling all morning and I see no end in sight. I need to go back upstairs," he had said curtly. His hair was damp and disheveled.

He had kissed her quickly on the cheek and dashed back into the elevator, leaving her to rub his kiss into her cheek. As he turned she had noticed that the back of his shirt was soggy with perspiration.

That was the last time she saw him.

At 4:05 p.m. that afternoon, five short minutes after the closing bell of the New York Stock Exchange had delivered a tortured intermission to a financially humbling day, her mother had picked her up at school, instead of her father.

At 4:58 p.m., her safe, calm, sheltered world came crashing down around her, with much sadder and grisly finality of a deeply personal nature that destroyed forever the life of casual and distant indifference that was ingrained into the core of a child born into great privilege and wealth on the Jersey Shore.

Tara calmly studied that elevator. Thank Heavens for her Happy Pills, she thought. One hundred and fifty milligrams a day. That's what it took her everyday to function normally, well, almost. The solitary fact that had haunted her every day was not so much how her father had died, but that he had died alone. There was no Dylan Thomas standing by her father's side as he died, exhorting 'Do not go gentle into that good night, William James'.

The doors pinged open, and for a brief, unnerving split second, the universe stood absolutely still, and a singular, crystal-clear albeit incongruous thought sparked through every cell in her body, from the crown of her head all the way down to the tips of her toes; *Daddy was going to emerge from the open doors of that elevator! Everything was going to be all right!* Every nerve tingled in a surge of uncontrolled anticipation, and her mouth went instantly dry.

But it was only a pimply young man with a mop of unruly, reddish hair; a trainee, judging by his ill fitting, washed white cotton button-down shirt, a pair of baggy cotton khaki, and a Princeton University tie.

Even her eyeballs shook as he stepped out of the elevator, in slow motion to her racing mind, and he did not even glance at her as he shuffled his way to the front doors.

The lump that had suddenly appeared in her throat stayed there. The only thing that she wanted to do was to heave, but she had a hunch that her knees were in no shape to carry her weight. She was startled at the ferocity of her panic attack, even though she had experienced such a vivid flashback before. This time around, she did not dare to allow herself a bout of prolonged, uncontrolled sobbing hysterics, and drew deep, modulated breaths to regain normal command, control and cognition.

Finally at 8:30 a.m., a tall, slender blonde in an indigo blue dress approached her. "Mr. Mulholland will see you now. Please follow me." She gave no indication if she had noticed anything out of the ordinary about Tara's countenance, and did not even make a customary offer of a drink of water, or coffee.

They took the elevator to the third floor, walked down an imposing corridor, and came to a massive set of wooden six-paneled doors. Tara was then ushered into a large windowless, featureless conference room that was dominated by an oversized laminated table. This was definitely not the mahogany-paneled boardroom where the financial desires of wealthy private clients were satisfied; this was the utilitarian room where pesky interlopers were curtly subdued and stripped of their personal dignity. Every large financial firm had at least one just like it.

Two men were seated at the far end. One was a pale, thin, balding man with a bright polka-dotted red bow-tie and suspenders. The second man, with a swarthy complexion, had aged since she had last seen him; he had been a pallbearer of her father's coffin, and had also delivered a very emotional eulogy. This was a soldier who had fought alongside her father in Vietnam.

Neither of the men stood up, and Tara immediately took note of that fact. She quietly seated herself around the corner from the bald person, who studied Tara, quite rudely she thought, for many long seconds. His mouth was tight, and he did not appear to have much in the way of lips. It was he who eventually broke the silence.

"I'm Mark Reuben, In-house Legal Counsel," he said, almost reluctantly, "and this is Mr. Mulholland, the Chief Executive." The swarthy man with the hair nodded briefly. The way Reuben referred to Mulholland with a 'Mr.' did not escape Tara.

"I'm Tara Morgan, as you know." She paused to see if the pained look on Reuben's face had deepened. It had.

Reuben scowled and pressed the fingers of both of his hands together in front of his lips. "Yes, we are quite aware of your background. And ... of course, Mr. Morgan, your father ..."

Tara looked straight at Reuben and met his cool gaze out of his pale water-blue eyes. Yes, she thought to herself, yes, you can say it. We all know what happened, don't we? She glanced at Mulholland, who was pointedly studying the blank pad of yellow paper in front of him. Definitely not a good sign at all.

Reuben addressed Tara, "Why are you here now?" Blunt and to the point. Very unfriendly.

Tara sat motionless in her chair, fighting her instincts to simply get up and leave. This was definitely not how it had played out in her mind. Her experience overruled her instincts by only an uncomfortably small margin, and she held Reuben's pointed gaze for a few seconds until he looked away with an expression deliberately of indifference even as she nodded her head in acknowledgement. Her instincts had obviously failed her; but she was clueless as to why they were being so mean and nasty to her. Did she have a tainted reputation of which she was unaware? She made a mental note to check with her friends on Wall Street.

But why indeed was she there? It was one that she had pondered over quite a few sleepless nights, but nevertheless had not been able to answer it to even her own satisfaction.

As improbable as it seemed even to her, she knew that at the crux lay an insatiable and unrealistic desire to bring her father back, to undo a moment in time that was irreversible. She became very creative at dreaming up events that would predicate the impossible, such as saying to herself on the basketball court at school, if I make this hoop he will return.

So there she was, on his hallowed ground. She had not even informed her mother that she had made any such overtures to her father's old company, since Isabella would have immediately put the kibosh on such a preposterous notion.

She turned her head toward Mulholland, who was still fixated on his pad, and spoke to him, ignoring Reuben. "As you know, I was at Goldman, Sachs in their Investment Banking Division, until September 11. That day, I realized that life was way too short, and took an unpaid leave of absence, for six months." She then directed her attention toward Reuben. "That expires on the 11th of March."

"I take it then that you don't have a desire to go back to them." Much to her surprise, it was Mulholland who asked that. His arms were resting on the table in front of him, but folded. On his left hand was a huge gold Rolex watch with a gold dial, which even his large physique could not dwarf. Unlike many whose Rolexes clunked about loosely, his was snug on his wrist.

"I would dearly love to go back to Goldman," she corrected him. "It's the City that I want to stay away from, after 9/11."

Mulholland asked "So you want to stay local, that's the reason why you want to work here?"

"Yes. And the fact that my father cofounded this firm. If he were still alive, he would have liked to see me here, I'm sure."

"Why did you not approach us when you got out of business school?" Mulholland again.

"I wanted to be established elsewhere," said Tara. Upon graduation, she had not wanted to ride in on her father's coattails, even though a decade had elapsed since his death. At the time she started in her freshman year at Wharton, she had little desire to even enter the world of finance. But like her mother, she followed the worldly news, and had a way of correlating seemingly unrelated bits of information into a logical whole that seemed to draw out their interdependencies. She could relate to historical events, human fears and dreams, and the immutable laws of nature, and provide rational explanations for the inconsistencies of life.

So like her father, she found her friends seeking her counsel on all matters under the sun. It became apparent to herself and Isabella that a rewarding career in finance or even law was very well within her reach. The secret toss of a coin with a co-conspirator sealed her fate; finance was in her destiny.

"What do you see yourself doing for us?" inquired Mulholland.

"Well, as you know, Central New Jersey has a lot of technology firms, especially in telecommunications. I see a lot of potential for incubating tech startups with a potential for success, as did my father before me."

Mulholland grimaced and shook his head. "That would have been a great business strategy five years ago, when the technology bubble started to gain steam." He firmly shook his head again. "You know the story since early 2001, the wayside is littered with the carcasses of Dot-Coms that became Dot-Gones."

"That's because most of the dot-coms did not have a business model that made any sense," said Tara.

"Anyway, this is truly a moot discussion," Reuben interrupted. "We have a strict policy of not hiring experienced outsiders. We hire directly from the best business schools, such as your own alma mater, Wharton. And that policy has worked very well for us so far."

"So you will not consider hiring me?"

Reuben shook his head. "No, not at all. As I said, we have a policy of not hiring outsiders." Evidently they had rehearsed their little routine in advance, for Reuben said, "The only reason we called you in was to avoid sending you an impersonal rejection letter, in deference to your late father. We will not hire you under any circumstances."

We will see about that, thought Tara, as she got to her feet.

Ramon DiCastro

Tuesday, January 29, 2002. Red Bank.

Ramon DiCastro leaned back in his burgundy leather high-backed swivel chair. True to form, it had been Tracey Avalon who had urged Tara to seek the legal counsel of Ramon, but had not clarified the nature of their relationship, leading Tara to speculate that it may not have been all about business. Trusting her friend's prodding, Tara had neglected to even check his field of specialty. It was not as if Tara did not know about lawyers; but she was looking for someone discreet, since her mother was not to know about her intentions.

Ramon's law practice was on Broad Street in a two-storied Victorian house that had been wholly converted into his office. There had been no sign outside indicating that it was even a law office, but Tracey had warned her in advance that it would be so, since he had no need to broadcast his presence.

The interior of the house had been gutted and professionally finished in rich paneled wood. In the lobby, there was a receptionist's cubby with a cherry writing desk, but it was unoccupied. There were no picture frames on his black walnut Sheraton desk, or anywhere in sight, which led her to wonder if his living quarters were upstairs. Judging by his crisp shirt and pressed suit, and a power tie, he had impeccable taste, and reeked of affluence. His smile was polite almost to the point of tolerant condescension. "Just to confirm what you have stated, Ms. Morgan, you went for an interview with the firm which your late father cofounded, you said. You sent a letter to one of the present partners."

"Jack Mulholland. He was a close friend of my father, and one of the original employees. He had served a tour in Vietnam together with my father."

"So that was a good choice then. Did Mr. Mulholland extend an invitation to meet?"

That was the strange part, for which she had no rational explanation. "No. My certified letter went ignored for a month. So I called his office about five or six times. Then one evening I called after the main switchboard was closed, and was able to reach him."

"That was certainly a clever idea. Then what happened?" he asked.

"He said hello, and that was it."

"Did you receive any indication that he recognized you?"

"Well, as soon as he answered the phone, I announced myself as Tara Morgan, daughter of William James Morgan III."

"I see. What was your sense? Was he pleased to hear from you?"

"No. He appeared a bit annoyed; probably because of the way I had bird-dogged him." She had her share of people jumping out of the woodwork and hitting her up for a job when she was at Goldman, Sachs. There were a lot of people from whom she hid as well as she could. So Mulholland's reticence was par for the course; after all he was the Chief Executive Officer.

"The fact remains that, you are the daughter of one of the cofounders of that firm. Did you have any contact with Mr. Mulholland while your father was alive?"

"I had seen him many times, while I was growing up. " He had come over to the house mostly for social events, dinners, her father's birthdays and even for breakfast once. Tara did not recollect ever seeing him with a significant other; he had always come by himself in one of many fastidiously gleaming black Cadillac cars that he favored, but seemed to invariably give a ride home to an unattached young lady.

"And after your father's demise?"

"I remember seeing him at the funeral." Then her mother had received him at the house one last time afterwards, and then no more. She did not recall ever seeing him at all since then, until her meeting of the prior week. Given the increasing fog that invariably accompanies the extended passage of time, Tara was not sure if her mother ever had the same kind of warm feelings for Mulholland that her father did.

In retrospect, it now seemed a bit odd to Tara that Mulholland did not have more prominence in her own childhood, notwithstanding that her mother had always been very reserved and private in her social interactions, in stark contrast to her father's bursting gregariousness.

Had there been some sort of a deep rift between Mulholland and Isabella? That would go a long way to explain his abrupt exit, and might even offer a shred of justification for his present rudeness. Or had he exhibited a lack of social grace even back then?

Even if she confronted Isabella about Mulholland, although she had no desire to do so, there was precious little anecdotal evidence to suggest that Isabella would actually shed any light on the topic. Many things were off-topic as far as her mother was concerned; one would have thought that her father's death would have brought Tara and her mother closer together, but in reality it only caused Isabella to turn off the light smile that she reserved only for her family, and to withdraw into a tighter shell. Tara did not relish the thought of subjecting her mother to anything that would revive memories of a very painful period of her life.

"Where did you go to school?" Ramon asked.

Tara knew that he was inquiring about her college education. "The Wharton School at the University of Pennsylvania."

"Right afterwards, probably even before you graduated, you were inundated with job offers, even from companies to which you had not applied, right?"

"Correct. Why this third degree, counselor?"

Ramon leaned back in his chair, a smug look spreading over his face. "Any jury comprised of poor working-class stiffs, would be easily forgiven for jumping to the conclusion that you had always led a very privileged life, sheltered especially because of your father's death. They would correctly guess, that you never had to ask for anything and all of your wishes and desires would be magically fulfilled for you, just like that." Thankfully he did not throw in a theatric snap of his long, thin fingers.

"A company certainly has the right to decide who is not a good candidate," said Tara calmly, stepping past the insult that had just been hurled her way. "Unless of course there is a very nice handy-dandy itsy-bitsy, teeny-weeny, little-known clause, written in fine-print in that aforesaid company's many Articles of Formation that clearly and unequivocally states that well-qualified children of past and present partners will be provided employment that is commensurate with their experience. Exactly what happens in a situation like that, counselor?"

Ramon shot straight up out of the swivel chair and almost leapt over the desk, alarming Tara that he might strike her in anger at her insolence. But his goal was only the empty chair next to her, and he sat down in it, after whipping it around to face her side. His eyes narrowed a bit. "There is actually a clause in their Articles of Formation that states that?"

"According to the copy that I have it most certainly does, counselor." She reached into her valise and pulled out the certificate of incorporation, which she held out for Ramon.

Ramon skimmed through relevant sections, looked up and nodded. "It appears that you may have a case."

Tara corrected him. "I have an undeniable right to get a job, in line with my experience, at Trundle, Morgan and Dickey."

"We will immediately pursue discussions with Morgan, Trundle and Dickey on the behalf of your father's estate."

Puzzled, Tara asked, "Why on the behalf of my father's estate, and not on my direct behalf?"

"If the case ever goes to trial, which I really doubt that it will, the jury will always try to accommodate the wishes of a departed person. Your father, after all, was a founding partner. His wishes are incorporated in this document. Are you married?"

"Recently divorced."

"The jury eats up divorced, white, attractive young women, especially if they have really cute kids.

"There is something else that you should know; my father was at the firm that afternoon when he shot himself in the head."

This Fish shall go to Heaven

I am really not interested in a serious relationship just now, Tara had reminded herself many times that day before Valentine's Day. Especially not with a guy whose days are literally quite totally numbered. Even though he is very cute and saved my Jamie's life. With the heavy heart that normally precedes a task much disliked but nevertheless quite necessary, Tara had picked up the cell phone and dialed Toby Roland's number to call off the dinner.

"Hi, Tara. What time are you going to pick me up?" Confident. Perky. Upbeat. Bubbly. Happy. Inviting. So full of death, and yet so full of life.

Tara shook her head. *Big mistake! Just say goodbye, and hang up, now, RIGHT NOW*!! "Where exactly is this restaurant anyway," squeaked out instead, and she closed her eyes and massaged her forehead while hearing him say that it was Moromisato's, a Japanese restaurant only a couple of blocks away from the Red Bank Train Station. It was not a fancy place, but almost a very well kept secret, and very authentic.

"But, it is Ash Wednesday," she regretfully pointed out. It marked the first day of the 46 days of Lent, which was observed by Roman Catholics by fasting, abstinence and penance.

"Ah, yes it is indeed!" he said. "You are allowed only one full meal today, which can be supplemented by 2 small meals that should not equal a full meal. So do make sure to only have a very light lunch. I would recommend nothing more than a small bowl of cereal, so that you do can stay in compliance. Of course dinner will be sushi, so we will be abstaining from meat. I have it all under control."

She had a feeling that he was teasing her for trying to pull religion. "Around six? What will you be wearing?" That slipped out completely unintentionally, for that was always a question she and Tracey would ask each other.

"Six-ish sounds good." Then she heard his boyish laugh that put her at ease. "That's the first time anyone asked me that. Will you be wearing your hooker-chic outfit again?"

"No." It was in the laundry, and even if it wasn't, there was no way that she would have even considered wearing it, just as she had no intention of wearing a big red ribbon either. "Remember ..."

"Yes, as I recollect, no serious relationship," he said, parroting her exact words on the boat. It was such a refreshing difference from her ex-husband who couldn't be bothered to remember stuff that had anything to do with her.

"Something very casual," she said.

"What? A very casual relationship?"

"I will wear something very casual," Tara replied dryly, not wanting to encourage his light banter, yet at the same time not wanting to appear aloof. Just a quiet dinner, nothing more.

ﾟﾟ ﾟﾟ ﾟﾟ ﾟﾟ ﾟﾟ

Of course, reality is usually far from one's imagination.

By half-past six that evening, they were seated across from each other at a low table, one of only a dozen, on thin tatami mats, their legs crossed underneath them.

Within moments of sitting down, a wave of fatigue washed over her. It had been quite a busy day, with the highlight being the noon Ash Wednesday Mass at the church. The choir had rendered the classic Miserere a Cappella. Using his fingers, dipped into ash formed to tradition by burning palm leaves from an earlier Palm Sunday, Father Clancy had then individually marked a cross into the congregants' foreheads. *Turn away from sin and be faithful to the Gospel,* had been his exhortation to each.

Even though her late afternoon shower had physically washed off the ashes, she could still feel its lingering presence, as though tattooed onto her forehead.

Tara specifically had not mentioned her looming dinner with Toby to her mother, or to Tracey, with whom she had spoken on the telephone. If Tara had not been disingenuous, she would have told Isabella that Tracey was actually calling from Paris, where she was spending a romantic getaway with her husband Walter; instead, Tara had merely informed her mother that she was going out to eat.

She knew that by doing so Isabella would be under the impression that her dinner companion was going to be Tracey, but she also felt that it was not any of Isabella's business as to with whom Tara had decided to dine that evening.

So it was with mixed emotions that Tara had slipped in that white lie, especially since she had done so on a holy day. On the whole, she rationalized that she was still a devout Catholic who recited the Lord's Prayer every single day, and had never missed even once, as far as she could remember.

She looked around surreptitiously at the other patrons to see if there were any familiar faces, but to her relief, there were not.

Catching herself drifting away in her reverie, with nothing to say, she asked him, more out of awkwardness than any real curiosity, "Do you have a girlfriend?" Might as well get that topic over with. She was curious since she had seen him pull out his cell phone earlier and set it to vibrate. Who was he expecting to call?

He smiled ruefully. "Not really! I just have the worst luck with pretty young girls. Look, case in point," he leaned forward, his hands punctuating the tale to follow, "Right after I graduated high school, I lived in Pittsburgh one summer."

Pittsburgh! Of all the places that he could have gone to, why Pittsburgh? Not to knock that big old city, thought Tara, but if she had a choice, she would have picked someplace like Hawaii. Then again, she had gone to Philadelphia when she herself could have attended college in Hawaii.

"I found myself a job putting up drywall in a skyscraper downtown," said Toby. "It was all full of union guys, but I managed to get a very decent wage, and it was far enough from home, but not that far away that I couldn't go back on a whim, you know?"

Tara perked up as Moromisato brought a pot of jasmine tea and poured it into two small cups. She offered Toby a handshake. "From one post high-school Pennsylvanian to another."

"What you drywalled skyscrapers, too?" laughed Toby.

She found it amusing too. "Attended the University of Pennsylvania."

"That's a great school, from what I hear," said Toby, "although downtown Philly is a very brutal place. I wouldn't go there myself. The school itself is great, but the surrounding area is nasty. Coming back to my story, I rented a little hole in the wall of an apartment. It was the greatest little hole in the wall, because it was mine, all mine."

Good for you, she thought. She had to share her dorm room with an unfriendly stranger because her mother would not let her live off campus. "Yes, please do continue," apologized Tara. "You were shinnying up some skyscraper in scenic downtown Pittsburgh, and … Oh, God! Please do not tell me that you ran into this great big honkin' chimp atop the skyscraper."

"No, that's a different movie, you plagiarist! I rented this little hole in the wall, and the night of my first day hard at work, I set my little white Westclox alarm clock, unrolled my sleeping bag, and happily lay down, all happy, and..."

"Wait! Wait!" said Tara, throwing all caution to the wind and paying no heed to the other patrons. "The phone rings. No, you don't have a phone yet. Have you been waiting all day for a telephone guy who doesn't show up, even though they promised to be there sometime between 9 and 5? Or somebody knocks at the door? That's it! It's a pizza guy, but he is not the real pizza delivery guy! He is actually some big ugly, mean dude who's just busted out of a max prison, snatched a delivery guy who wandered into the wrong alley, ripped off his clothes, and now wants a pretty white country boy to keep him company!"

Toby waved his hands in protest. "That sounds like that could be your story. But there's no wild-eyed fake pizza delivery man in my story." He paused to refill Tara's teacup from the pot of jasmine tea before pouring some for himself. "But there is a flaw in your story, though. When your dude grabbed the pizza guy, he got his pretty white country boy. Why would he come looking for me?"

"I see your point. That's why you are a successful officer of the law," said Tara. She thanked him for refilling her cup of tea. It was just something every man would do for a lady, or should do so if his mama raised him right, and apparently his did, thought Tara, taking a sip of the fragrant, steaming beverage. "Ok, so it's not a pizza guy at the door. Go on."

"No, I hoped it was a pizza delivery guy! Anyway, it's not as if somebody was at the door. It's this wail, this loud, mournful *owooooooooo* of some huge Hound of the Baskervilles, emanating from the apartment right next to mine. That dog howled the whole night!"

"Why didn't you bang on the wall, or shout out, or something?"

"I had no idea who occupied the apartment next door. For all I knew, it could have been the fake pizza guy from your story! Who now has a gun, or worse, a cleaver freshly stained with red human blood. So this homeboy stayed put, like his daddy taught him, wide awake and cursing the whole night, or at least until 3:30 a.m., when that infernal hound finally shut up."

"And of course you had to wake up at five and go to work drywalling, right?" offered Tara.

"It's almost like you were there, Tara! How did you know that?" he said, his eyes bulging in mock exaggeration. "Which is exactly what I had to do, so there was no way I could see who was living there. Continuing on with my tale, after work, I grab a burger and a beer, and reluctantly walk back home at eight, and every thing's very quiet. So I turn the light off and lie down…"

"Owoooooooo!" Tara burst out, laughing.

"Owoooooooo is right! All night long! Again, it was past three by the time that darn mutt cut that nonsense out. Thankfully, the next day was Saturday, so I could sleep in. But I wake up at seven like I always do, and get dressed to go get some coffee. So I open the door, and my neighbor is standing outside her door."

"Aha! So it was a she," exclaimed Tara. "Was she an exotic-looking lass from Tahiti in a grass skirt and coconut shells? Or perhaps a comely young French maid in a skimpy black outfit with white lace frills? Or a stripper from Tuskegee in her stage outfit? What was she?"

Toby leaned forward with a wistful gleam. "She was the most innocent-looking girl I had ever laid eyes on. She was hardly a day over seventeen and she looked as pure as the morning dew, fresh as a Pennsylvania country morning. All rural milk-and-corn-fed country gal!" He inhaled deeply. "She was definitely God's personal hand-maiden. Her skin was so radiant, with pale skin, cheeks a beautiful pink, she was a porcelain doll."

"You are drooling all over your nice shirt," said Tara, slightly miffed.

"So she lays her dewy eyes on me, and I instantly melt away. She says her name is Vera Ann, and sorry, but her dog Buster's been very sick, and she hopes that his howling hadn't disturbed my sleep."

"Of course like a fool you shook your head No, right?"

"Of course! The net story is that she has to go to work."

"As a stripper?" Tara needled.

"No, she worked at JC Penney of all things, 2nd floor women's intimate apparel or something like that, and had to be at work that Saturday. So she asks me if I mind taking Buster to the vet while she goes off to her job."

"How about that! Of course you jumped at Vera Ann's request," said Tara.

"Of course I did. What red-blooded American wouldn't? Vera Ann digs into her pocket, pulls out twenty bucks, hands me the vet's card, and says she will get the precious pooch all ready. So I go back inside to get my car keys, and a few minutes later when I open the door, there's this immense fluff-ball of a mutt with long, dirty shaggy hair standing outside my door, with his massive tail swishing back and forth. I look around, and there's no Vera Ann, so I says Buster, let's go."

"Naturally the stupid dog stays put..." ventured Tara.

"So you were there!" exclaimed Toby with a laugh. "Yeah, of course the stupid dog stays put. But I grew up on a farm, and even though I didn't have my trusty cattle prod, I grabbed Buster's collar and walked him out, and literally stuffed him into my pickup truck's tiny cab."

"Naturally the mutt had to stand sideways sticking his head out the window, so you got a lovely scenic view of his smelly butt."

"You so know dogs!" Toby wagged a finger at her.

"Yes, I have three wonderful German Shepherds. Been there, done that."

"So we make the rounds to the vet, who examines him, says there's really nothing wrong with him, and gladly takes the twenty bucks, and sends us on or merry way."

"What did you do with the dog afterwards? Did Vera Ann give you the keys to her apartment?" asked Tara.

"I wish, but no joy. So Buster and I went to a park that I had spotted, we spent an hour playing, and then he looked quite dirty, to tell you the truth. So I dug into my pockets and paid to get him shampooed and stuff at some pet grooming place that the vet had recommended, and took him back to my apartment shortly after 1."

"So by three p.m. you were happily bedding a grateful and nubile Vera Ann."

"Now I can tell you really were so not there!" Toby laughed. "When I get back, I find Vera Ann opening the door to her apartment, and she has this intensely cross look on her face."

"Why? Because you had the dog groomed without telling her?"

Toby refilled her teacup again, trying hard to compose himself. "No. I had the wrong darned dog!"

"What?" Tara gasped, raising her hand to her mouth.

"That's right. I had the wrong darned dog! Apparently it belonged to some old biddy down the hall. Poor Vera Ann had waited a whole hour for me to show up, and when I didn't, went knocking on my door, and when I was no-where to be found, she had to call in sick, lost a day's wages at JC Penney, had to take Buster, the real one, to the vet herself, and so on and so forth. Needless to say, she was very disappointed in me."

Tara shook her head in disbelief. "No way!"

"Yes way. So Vera Ann never really cottoned on to me after that, and one day at the end of summer she quietly moved away."

"Good old Vera, gone and never to be heard from again. Reminds me of that old Pink Floyd song, Vera! Vera! What has become of you?"

"That was Vera Lynn," corrected Toby.

"That was quite some story," she said. "I'm sorry that it ended that way. A tragic ending with a tinge of a promising beginning, but with absolutely no joy in between. But I bet that old biddy was pretty grateful for what you did. Did she at least put you in her will?"

Toby sighed. "With my luck, she will live a thousand years if she had, which she didn't."

Moromisato brought and placed on the table a bowl with what was obviously a root, and a wooden paddle that had some kind of grey material attached to its wide end.

Tara learned that it was wasabi root, known colloquially known in Japan as namida or tears. That green pasty stuff normally served at Japanese restaurants was really colored horseradish that they scraped out of a crusted jar, said Toby.

That chunk of root in front of them was known as hon-wasabi, or true wasabi.

"What do you do, gnaw on it?" Tara asked him.

Smiling off her needle, he pointed to the paddle. "We grate the hon-wasabi on the same-gawa. Go ahead".

"What's this *we* stuff? You bring me to a restaurant so we can prepare our own meal?" But even as she was saying it, Tara picked up the paddle, and touched the grey material, which was extremely coarse, like a piece of rough sandpaper.

"It's sharkskin, the traditional way to grate hon-wasabi," said Toby.

Tara gingerly held the root by the thick end and started to rub the thin end back and forth. Toby reached over and flipped the hon-wasabi so that the thick end was against the sharkskin. "The thick end is where the growth is still occurring, and is the freshest part. They strongly recommend a circular motion."

That made sense. "Are you sure that a Japanese geisha named Suki shouldn't be the one to do this, instead of a Yankee gai-jin?" Immediately, she regretted sounding churlish.

"The Japanese way is that anything worth doing is worth doing correctly, and well." He peered into the bowl a few minutes later, and nodded in satisfaction. "Let's set that aside for a few minutes to let it resolve any harshness."

So this is how he spent his two-year ticket in Japan, courtesy of the US Marines? Chowing down on sushi? "I would hazard a guess that they didn't serve hon-wasabi in the marine Mess Halls of Okinawa. How did you become a sushi connoisseur, and how did you learn to speak Japanese?"

Toby's eyes grew a bit narrower. "Stuff happens."

Moromisato returned shortly with a steaming hot towels neatly arranged on a bamboo stand. Toby took Tara's hand in his and wiped off her fingers with a hot towel. "Let me know if this oshibori is too hot." Tara was taken by surprise at his chivalrous gesture. Then he did the same with her other hand. "Did you ever eat Ikezukuri?" he asked.

No, she hadn't heard of it. It didn't sound very edible, but it was a pristine form of sashimi, was the assurance that Toby offered.

Moromisato came back with a large plate, which was an elaborate setting that showcased a large, whole fish, seemingly intact, whose head and tail arced up, skewered together, from the plate.

Tara's mouth went suddenly dry. "Look at the skin, so iridescent! The fish seems so alive! Are you sure it's really not?"

"Have you ever eaten raw oysters that have been freshly shucked?" asked Toby. "This is very similar. It's very fresh sushi. Moromisato selected it and prepared it for us."

Moromisato extracted a pair of chopsticks from his pocket and merely grazed the skin of the carp, and to Tara's horror, the entire side flicked away, revealing its insides, with vertical lines where Moromisato's sharpest knife had sliced and diced the gutted fish, whole, into bite-sized strips of sashimi. She almost expected the pieces to be quivering with life, but thankfully they were not.

Tara became aware that Toby and Moromisato were watching her intensely. She had eaten lots of sushi and sashimi before, as well as ceviche and even steak tartare, although the last was on one occasion only. It was not so much solely the rawness of the fish, but that it was raw and seemingly still on the fish, although she knew that it must have been filleted, cleansed, sliced and meticulously placed back on the carcass.

"Now I understand," said Tara. "It's a very pristine form of sashimi, indeed."

"Yes," smiled Moromisato. "Japanese lore has it that if the eater likes the Ikezukuri, the fish will go to heaven." With that, Moromisato used the tips of his chopsticks and picked up a piece of the fish. Smearing a bit of the fresh hon-wasabi, he dipped the clean end of the sashimi in the shoyu sauce and held it in front of Tara.

She attempted to reach for it with her own chopsticks. Toby immediately corrected her, "People in Japan use the hashi to pass something only at a funeral." This time, Tara opened her mouth, and Moromisato placed the morsel on her tongue.

"I have never tasted sashimi that fresh and flavorful," she said. "Yes. This fish is most definitely going to heaven." The wasabi and the soy sauce were unlike anything she had ever savored.

Moromisato nodded his thanks, and acknowledged that his cousins supplied the shoyu sauce from the Izu peninsula of the Shizuoka prefecture in Japan, where they also personally grew the hon-wasabi. The music was quite exquisite, and she learned that the artist was Kitaro, a Japanese New Age musician and the album was called India.

Toby had selected a piece for himself, and chewed and swallowed it before saying that Ikezukuri sashimi was always chewier than what one is accustomed to in a local Japanese restaurant where the fish is most certainly not fresh, and most likely has been frozen. Toby offered up a pink piece of pickled ginger, Gari, and Tara ate it to cleanse her palate. Ikezukuri does not have time to go through rigor mortis, which causes the flesh to go limp. "This is still tense from its ending," he said.

Tara glanced fleetingly at the fish on the plate. It was, she decided, probably very close to the ending, but it certainly did not appear to be entirely in heaven just yet. Maybe a flicker of gill or two away from there, but seemed as if all it needed was to be wrapped up in a bit of seaweed and thrown back into the water for it to go about happily on its way.

She reached for the small cup of hot sake at the side, and took a diversionary sip of the searing wine.

"Ikezukuri is reserved for very special occasions to honor the guests," he said. In Japan, authentic Ikezukuri was really live fish that has been stunned and very quickly carved up, so it was not quite dead yet. He had one which was still gasping by the time they had finished consuming it. Tara was relieved to find out that in the States, it was served like the carp on the table, and not alive.

He had dated a Japanese girl, he finally admitted with reluctance. That was how he came to know so much about their ways. Tara could tell it was still very painful, and placed her hand on his. It seemed to be a natural thing to do. He held Tara's hand very gently, caressing her palm with his thumb.

Her family was from a small fishing village, and was very traditional. They had not cared for her daughter to be dating a gaikoku no kata, which was a very polite way to say foreigner, rather than the very derogatory gaijin, which would not be used in polite circles.

Marines rely on the Navy for medical services; by the time the Naval physician had discovered his cancer, Toby had become even less desirable in her parents' eyes. So he had done the right thing and left.

To Tara, that seemed to be a very honorable thing for him to do. "Did they relent and plead for your forgiveness? Did you go back to her?"

Toby shook his head. "No. They did not try to stop me, and even if they had, I would have not reconsidered my decision to leave their daughter alone." It was a matter of personal honor and principle, he said simply. That was the way he had been raised, and that was what he had taught in the Marines. Never do anything to dishonor your God, your country, your family, your comrades and yourself.

You are certainly a very honorable and good man, Charlie Brown, Tara thought, locking her fingers into his. By the time Moromisato appeared again, they had eaten through all of the sashimi. He took the platter away, and returned about ten minutes later with a bowl of soup.

"Hmm, fish-head soup," Tara raised her eyebrows. The head of the carp that had been looking as if it had been gasping for water half an hour ago was finally back in water, but no longer faking to be still alive, however feebly, and was no longer even attached to its skeleton, however bereft of any flesh or organs. It simply floated incongruously appetizing on its side among pieces of tofu and finely chopped scallions in a clear, fragrant broth.

"Oh, an added bonus!" Toby pointed to a small bowl filled with tiny black, glittering balls.

Tara could not bring herself to eat the roe, although she had eaten caviar many times, standing at the kitchen sink. The Jewish custom of Kosher, not eating milk with the meat that it had nourished, and of not eating the eggs with the poultry that had borne them, came into sharp focused realization. Toby, on the other hand, had no such compulsion, and attacked the roe with ferocity while their mother, or at least her cleanly severed head, looked on at him, helplessly bobbing up and down like an ignored buoy.

He had ladled some of the broth, tofu and scallions into two soup bowls and handed one to Tara. She accepted it, grateful that he had not plunked the fish head into her bowl.

But she watched aghast as he reached in with the tapered end of his hashi and pried the eyeball out of its socket. Tara knew that the look of horror on her face did not elude Toby, for he did not offer her the eyeball. Instead, he popped it into his mouth. She watched his Adam's apple rise and quickly fall as the gelatinous organ slid down his throat.

Curiosity eventually got the better of her, and she ventured to claw at the jowls to pick off a small piece. She carefully swished it around in the broth and snared a green ring of scallion. The flesh was very tender, as she had expected, and dissolved in her mouth. It was delicious. Her mother had spoken of eating fish-head soup while she was growing up, but she had never tried any herself.

"Must not ever have been hungry enough," said Toby dryly. "It's a curse of being an affluent American. We are trained to be selective, such as eating no organ meats, nothing that has more than four legs, yada yada yada. People in other countries do not waste any of the animal whose remains they are consuming. Personally, it's an insult to the poor creature if you do not have the courtesy of consuming all of it, I think."

"Yes, not to mention its one thousand unborn seeds," said Tara. "How were they, by the way?"

Their dinner ended with fresh, juicy raspberries, which they washed down with sweet Japanese plum wine. Tara reached for her purse, but Toby shook his head. This was his good friend Moromisato's treat.

"Do you want to walk up Broadway? Or do you have to leave?" asked Toby as they stepped away from the warmth of the restaurant and into the bitterly cold night.

Tara shivered. "If we pick up a bottle of wine and go back to your boat, will you have a *get out of jail free* card for me?" She knew it was more than the sake talking.

"Remember, no serious relationship," Toby playfully nudged her, and pulled something out of his pocket. "Moromisato slipped me the Kitaro CD that you so liked."

He was such an optimist, she thought, slipping her hand into Toby's and raising her face. "Happy Valentine's Day."

St. Valentine's Day

Thursday, February 14, 2002. Middletown.

In 1969, three years before Tara was born, the Roman Catholic Church had stopped observing St. Valentine's Day on its calendar, citing a lack of clear historical record. Her mother had never managed to get over the decision of the Church, and continued to honor it solely by going to church. So unlike many of her own generation, Tara had never really known St. Valentine's Day as a gift-giving holiday. Further, the notion of gifting jewelry, a recent practice initially instigated by the diamond industry, as a Valentine's Day gift was conspicuously absent in the Morgan household.

So that particular Thursday would have normally transpired as any other day, save for a brief trip to church, had it not been for a series of major events that took place in domino fashion. The first was of course that she had committed the cardinal sin of lust, *luxuria* as Dante Aligheri had called it, on Ash Wednesday, the Day of Repentance, of all days, with only a modicum of genuine remorse, not a shred of it of religious roots. The second transgression came because she had not simply engaged in fornication, but in the eyes of the Catholic Church she had committed adultery.

Interestingly enough, her remorse had first signaled its displeasure only when Toby had started to suckle at the tips of her breasts, the same that had nourished Jamie. At that juncture, she could simply have rebuffed his infringement, packed up and left; but she had not.

The singular emotion that had surged through her psyche was one of pure emancipation; indeed, it was an instantaneous liberation from the rightful anger and resentment that she had henceforth bottled up and carried within herself after the initial shock of seeing her ex-husband in bed with his concubine.

This was serious payback time, she had successfully convinced herself, that would right that horrible wrong that had been inflicted on her innocence by her ex-husband. She had welcomed Toby Roland's advances, and it was her lack of inhibitions and her cavalier attitude that had disturbed her the most on the drive home.

Her anguish lay in that time and again during her young life, she had been an innocent victim of circumstances that were totally beyond her control, for which she was mere collateral damage. Here she had always been, minding her own business, when whammo! Plague and pestilence kept striking at her. If she was to keep getting punished, then, she reasoned, she may as well commit the crime.

The worst had come her way right after her father's death. Until then she had led a very privileged childhood, but when compared to those of the kids of neighboring Rumson, hers had been a fairly unremarkable one. There were neither summers at the Cape, nor winters skiing in Utah; in the eyes of her parents, the Jersey Shore had all that they needed. Their self-effacing bonhomie ensured a good stream of friends, most of whom vanished after his death.

She knew of a few rich kids of the area whose fathers had gone to jail for various sundry white-collar crimes, but at least they could draw strength and solace from the undeniable fact that they would eventually be reunited with their sires. Not so in her case, for she knew that he wasn't coming back.

As a teenager, it would have been a bearable tragedy to have a parent die; to die by his own hand was an entirely different trauma, for how could she even begin to explain away such a terrible deed? To a whole gaggle of sadistic tormentors looking for even the slightest pretext to claw someone, anyone, down, she was now fresh red meat in bloodied waters, without anyone rushing to her rescue.

In his childhood too, her father had been the subject of many cruel taunts from his schoolmates. How come his daddy had died in World War II when their own had returned, even if not fully intact? Wasn't he a good enough soldier? How many Nazis had he killed before he was shot out of his ineptitude?

What does one say in repartee? That it didn't matter how many Nazis he had killed, but that he had sacrificed his own one and only life in the service of his country, the one that he loved? Would the deaths of unknown, unseen and equally unfortunate enemy soldiers bring back his own father, whose dinner plate would forever remain empty, even as it presently remained in the display cabinet of the fallen soldier's granddaughter and her daughter? What happens when in the process of trying to make the other soldier die for his country you happen to die for yours?

Her father eventually had joined the Marines in honor of his father, to defend him, to prove that his supreme sacrifice would never go unheeded. He just needed to walk in his father's footsteps, to see what that soldier had seen, but could never pass on to the son that he would never see.

The forces of turmoil continued into her adult life. Here she was, a young mother with child who possessed a sickness that was difficult for others to really comprehend.

Added to that, how could she explain away the sordid episode of her ex-husband in bed with the baby-sitter? So it was into dark shell that she had retreated.

By any yardstick, she was definitely very lonely, and had been especially so in the waning days of her marriage. But in reality it was not as if she was easy due solely to that loneliness, but she had been genuinely impressed by his openness, honesty and his conversations.

He had made her feel once more like a woman being courted, and that she was very special. His subsequent lovemaking had been exquisite; the waters of the Navesink River had been seasonally rough and she had wondered whether the rocking of the boat, punctuated by muffled booms of distant thunder and outbursts of cold, pelting rain backlit by subdued lightning, with a few creaks rumbling through the old superstructure of the wharf, was in reality the collective, muted wrath of the Gods or just their grudging applause.

Back in her own bed, she had woken up with a start quite a few times during the night, her mind replaying snippets of their lovemaking, but she had managed to go right back to sleep without any problems, her skin still tingling with the memory of his caresses, his scent deliciously lingering on her body.

A long, hot shower after finally waking up to start her day had assuaged any lingering guilt that she may have harbored, and left her in very good spirits to fend off any rebuke from her mother. Why had she not done this sooner, she wondered with her first natural, unfettered smile in over half a year.

It was half-past nine in the morning, and Jamie had already eaten, but was quite ready for more. Tara toasted two frozen homemade egg- and dairy-free waffles before slathering them with marmalade. "Is that good?" asked Tara, realizing too late that she already knew her daughter's very predictable response.

"You always ask me that," Jamie replied, not out of curtness, but just matter of factly; she did not favor pleasantries. In her mind, there was no reason for that waffle to be anything but good.

"There's more," said Tara, always happy to see her daughter eat.

"Yes, I know that." Nana had gone outside to fetch the newspaper, Jamie informed her, perched on a stool at the kitchen table. Moreover, she continued without taking her eyes off Tara, in the flat tone that she reserved to display her displeasure, the dogs had to be fed.

Tara nodded, wondering who was the parent there. But she definitely knew the source of Jamie's hurt. "Did you miss me yesterday night?"

Without saying a word, Jamie slid off the stool and retreated into the living room, her shoulders slumped. Tara decided to give her a few minutes alone, and poured herself a cup of coffee.

"Mommy, I see a truck pulling up," said Jamie.

Tara did not recall having ordered anything, so she went to investigate, and peering through the glass, saw a white truck bearing the banner of a local florist. She opened the door and stepped out onto the covered porch that ran all around the house. The delivery man pulled out a huge, long box and came up to the stairs. "Tara Morgan? Please sign here."

Tara scribbled on the electronic tablet and extracted the envelope before handing Jamie the box. She had a good notion as to who had sent them. Sliding her forefinger under the flap, Tara ripped it open and read the card, with her initial amusement changing instantly to revulsion when she saw the sender's name. "Jamie, this is a mistake. These are not for us! Bring the box back!" she said.

"No, mommy. You are mistaken. They are for us, from Daddy." The calm deliberateness of her tone caused Tara to look at her. Jamie's normally calm face was distorted so grotesquely out of proportion to her tone that Tara had to look away in horror, shaken and flabbergasted. Then Jamie began to spew obscenities and epithets that were chillingly verbatim sound bites that Tara distinctly remembered having exchanged with Todd Scott Preston during the final days of their marriage.

Upon hearing Jamie's choice words, Tara immediately had a good grasp of what it must really feel to be hit in the face by a two-by-four. Hyphenated or otherwise, it had to hurt.

"No, Jamie. They are not for us. We have to give them back. We are not keeping them! Please do as I say." Flustered, Tara glanced at the delivery guy, who just got into the truck and drove away.

"Jamie, I am sorry. I was mistaken," Tara tried to cover. But the hurt in Jamie's eyes tore at her heart, and Tara knelt down on the wooden floor. "I am truly sorry, Jamie. Come to Mommy, please, sweetheart."

Isabella came around the porch from the back of the house. "What was all that ruckus about?"

"Daddy sent us a big box of roses!" said Jamie, casting a disapproving glance at Tara. "But Mommy did not appreciate it."

"We can talk about it later," said Isabella. Tara knew that it was not a ruse to distract Jamie, but Isabella's normal way to defuse the situation until it could be discussed calmly. Tara also noticed that Isabella was looking directly at her, and not at Jamie. Then, "Do you want to come to church with me, Jamie?"

Going to church was definitely out of the question for Tara, since she needed to go to Confession first, and there just was no time. Technically, she could go and attend the Mass, but she could not receive Communion, and it would be quite obvious to everyone that she had committed some sort of sin. "You two go ahead, I'll just stay home and bake some cookies," said Tara.

Right after Isabella and Jamie left, Tara dialed the loathed number. Bounce to voice mail. Thank God. She left a calm message to her ex-husband, demanding that he never ever send her any flowers again, unless it was for her funeral. In case he had any questions, she said, all that he had to do was to read the divorce agreement that he had signed, and to pay attention to the section where he agreed specifically to make no further contact with Tara, Jamie or Isabella.

This was her first contact with Todd since the divorce, and she had really braced herself for something like that to happen over Christmas, but gratefully it had not. Why would he reach out to her the day after she had finally liberated herself from him, let alone on Valentine's Day? The card bore no evidence of any sentiment on his part, and merely had his name, signed no doubt by a clerk at the florist. She was more angry than hurt, taking this unforeseen event as a ding for her sins of the prior night, reminding her that in the eyes of the church, she was still married to that unworthy lout. Only God puts asunder what He has joined together in holy matrimony; and He puts asunder by death. That was that.

ᕤ ᕤ ᕤ ᕤ ᕤ

Her ex-husband called five times, without leaving a message, and each time she had calmly ignored the call. The sixth time, she was ready to set it to mute, when she looked at the display, which flashed a local number in the 732 area code. It was the florist. He said that he had another delivery for her, and was calling to see if she was accepting any more deliveries, before he made the trip.

"I am terribly sorry," said Tara. "I do apologize for my behavior earlier. But yes, please do drop them by." And this time around, she made sure to have a tip ready for him.

ભ ભ ભ ભ ભ

Later, she heard Toby Roland's gentle laugh on the phone. "I hope I didn't cause any trouble by sending flowers your way, Tara."

"No, thank you very much. But I did receive some definitely unwanted ones from my ex earlier in the day, though." Tara suddenly realized that Toby had thus far not asked her about a significant other. "But you didn't know if there was someone…."

"Ouch. Sorry. Well, I figured you were not the kind of person to cheat on your nearest and dearest. Being a cop I see all kinds and you definitely did not seem to be anything but a very nice girl."

"But even in light of last night?" she teased. It's still not a serious relationship with Toby, she reminded herself.

"Especially in light of last night. Look, do you have any regrets? Please do say no, in that delicious voice of yours."

"Not really," she said with a laugh. "But I will not go so far to say that I don't have any regrets."

"Some regrets, then? Me too. I regret that I made you do something that you would regret. My bad. I wish I could turn the clock back on that."

"Really? Or are you just saying that?"

"Marine's honor, ma'am. Where do we go from here?" His tone was solicitous, but that did not cover the fact that he was forcing her to face the issue at hand. But she only had herself to blame, for having been so forthright in the first place. She could just as well have claimed to be ridden with guilt, and that she could never see him again, and he would probably have understood.

Yes, where indeed? Tara sat down on the couch, her mouth abruptly dry and her heart thumping under her sweater. She vaguely smelt her own fear. She had not anticipated the complications that she had brought upon herself, but there was no right answer.

She desperately needed his attention, but to what end? How does one embrace the notion of starting a relation-ship of any kind with a terminally ill person? She un-derstood the silliness of that question, for every living thing is in the process of dying. His process was just being sharply accelerated. It would have been quite different, she thought, if they were already in love, and then his disease was diagnosed. If he was damaged goods, then so was she. He had a right to love, and be loved, as did she.

She recalled her wedding vows, in sickness and in health. How could she plunge into taking care of another bird with a broken wing when she was already all tapped out? Finally there was the little adultery clause that had to be worked out with the church, regardless of with whom she locked lips.

"It's not easy," she finally said. "But then again, I am not the one dying of cancer." She did not realize what she had said until after the words spilled out in a stream of consciousness. Her own transparency alarmed her, for she normally preferred to be noncommittal, but after an evening spent doing various unmentionable but gratifying things to each other, what other options did she have?

"Is that what's troubling you?" Again, she liked that he was inquiring about her thoughts.

"Yes. I would be lying if I pretended otherwise, Toby."

"Good bye, Tara." He just hung up.

Tara rocked back and forth in her corner of the couch. What the hell was she thinking? She did not know him that well, after all, other than in the Biblical sense, to confess her deepest thoughts. Then she called him back.

"Yes." Cold. Flinty.

"Toby …. I said that's what is troubling me. I don't think my honesty should anger you."

"I am not angry. I have too limited a time ahead for anger. I just do not want to fritter it over regrets. I will have all eternity for that."

Tara choked. "I'll have to call you back!" The lump in her throat ballooned very sharply, leaving her breathless. She jumped to her feet, and frantically gulped for air, salty tears cascading down the side of her nose and cheeks, and pooling at the corners of her mouth.

The phone rang, and she answered it without looking at the number.

"Hello, Tara." It was Todd Scott Preston.

Without even uttering a single sound she just hurled the phone across the room. Throwing on a short coat, she grabbed her keys and ran out to the Porsche. As the 6-cylinder engine throatily rasped into eager life, she mashed the throttle, sending a spray of gravel clunking against the fenders. Coming out of her driveway, the rear tires clawed furiously at the road, and in a couple of heartbeats the speedometer jumped to 65. As she reached to shift into third, the bellow of a police siren behind her startled Tara. Oh no!

She pulled over and rolled the window down as the Middletown police officer vigilantly and deliberately approached her car, his service revolver ominously drawn.

"License and registration, please, ma'am."

Tara forced herself to look away from the barrel of the gun and looked in alarm at the empty seat next to her. "Officer, I left my purse at home, over there." She timorously jabbed a finger at her house, hardly half a mile down the road.

"I saw you come out of that house driving with reckless abandon, ma'am. You could have caused serious damage not only to yourself, but to others, especially when I clocked you at over 60 miles per in a residential neighborhood with many young children." With a deliberate flourish, he engaged the safety and re-holstered the gun.

Wiping the tears off her face, she said meekly, "I am terribly sorry, officer."

"Seeing as you probably had a rough day, I will just ticket you for driving without a license if you will turn around and follow me back to your house. And do not leave your house again until you regain control of yourself, got it?"

"Yes, sir. Thank you, officer." She knew that she would have to go to court and demonstrate that she had a valid license, and the ticket would be dismissed without any points accumulating against her driving record. So it was a very kind concession that the officer had made.

ભ ભ ભ ભ ભ

By the time the officer had written up the ticket and left, Isabella and Jamie arrived. As Tara stepped out of the house to greet them, still wearing her coat, she saw the nose of a Red Bank police cruiser outside her gate. "Ma, I will be right back. Take Jamie inside," said Tara and she quickly walked up to the cruiser. Behind the wheel, she spotted Toby, alone. She approached his open window.

"You should listen to the police radio," he said. "They were just talking about a very upset pretty young thing on River Road in Middletown that shot like a bat out of hell in a Porsche 911 Turbo, without her license."

"Guilty as charged, officer," Tara slumped her shoulders, raising one arm up lackadaisically, and pouted her lower lip.

Isabella came up on them. "Is everything OK?" Then she recognized Toby. "Oh, you are the officer who saved Jamie."

Toby got out of the car. "Yes, ma'am. Just a courtesy call to see how she is doing."

"Oh, she is doing just fine!" replied Isabella. "She's inside icing some cookies. Why don't you come in for a few and some coffee?"

"Yes, why don't you?" asked Tara sweetly.

❧ ❧ ❧ ❧ ❧

It was past nine that night by the time Jamie finally began to settle down for her bedtime routine. After Tara had beseeched her for the third time to put on her pajamas, the little scamp had tied the long sleeves of her one-piece fleece pajamas around her neck, and tied the legs around her waist, like a backpack. "I do have my pajamas on," she sang out. Tara knew that Jamie was still on a sugar rush from scarfing down all the cookies, so she stifled a laugh and cut her a bit of slack.

For the first time in a couple of months, Tara had been interested enough to pick up the newspaper. She had been reading an article in the newspaper that the U.S. Government Printing Office, citing the usual post-9/11 reasons, had ordered librarians to destroy copies of CDs that contained some reference materials about public water supplies. Just so that she could finish the article, Tara went back downstairs.

"Those are very nice pajamas that you got Jamie," said Tara, pouring out two cups of decaffeinated tea for Isabella and herself. Jamie had a growth spurt that left all of her winter pajamas from the prior year suddenly quite short. Tara had been meaning to replace them, but had not done so yet.

"What's going on in your life, Tara?" said Isabella after Tara had poured

Tara picked up the newspaper. "Whatever do you mean, Ma?"

"You never were a good sneak," said her mother. "Was the officer really just dropping in to see how Jamie was doing?"

"Why not?" asked Tara innocently.

"You tell me. A Red Bank policeman drives all the way up to Middletown to drop in and check up on a young girl at 4:30 p.m. on Valentine's Day afternoon. And, you sauntered in during the wee hours this morning. By the way, who sent you those other flowers? You tell me, daughter."

"I am a grown woman, Ma." Tara sniffed.

"I want you to talk to a psychologist," said Isabella.

"That's a good idea," said Tara. "I'll call around tomorrow and make an appointment for Jamie."

"You are the one who needs help," said Isabella.

Vinca Dinca Pinca

Wednesday, February 27, 2002. Red Bank.

At 9:00 a.m., as planned the prior evening, Tara arrived at The Flaky Tart but she had to wait for almost half an hour before Toby Roland showed up, still in his uniform.

"Sorry to have kept you waiting," he said.

That was quite all right, she said, knowing that he had worked the overnight shift.

As they picked their coffee, he hunkered down and squinted at the large labels on the clear mason jars of coffee beans. "Look at this label; House Blend, Costa Rican Vinca Dinca Pinca something; a lightweight champion with a firm well rounded body. Sure sounds like the gal of my dreams. But still, which marketing genius came up with that mouthful, anyway?"

"I've never had that before," said Tara, looking at the label, which really said Juan Vinas Estate. "Is that what you are going to have?"

"After working the graveyard shift I can see myself with a firm, well rounded body," said Toby with a wink, "but that will have to wait until after we eat." They did have a date to do exactly that.

"Funny you should say that," said Tara, reaching up and tugging on his tie to make him come closer, only to have it snap right off. "And which grammar school do *you* attend, little boy," she said, pointedly cradling the limp clip-on tie in the palm of her hand.

"It's meant to come off for my safety," said Toby. "Just so a bad guy doesn't grab it, yank real hard and pop me on the nose. You were saying?"

"I spoke with my attorney Ramon on my way over," she said, after they sat down.

"Thrill me. Did any good come out of it?"

She leaned in closer, and tried her best imitation of a movie vamp. "Well, my dahlin', he ... shall we say ... got me feeling quite naughty, if you get my drift."

"Isn't there a law against an attorney doing that to his client," Toby asked with a twinkle in his eye. "Oh, what am I saying, of course they don't have to worry about a tiny little pedestrian nuisance such as ethics getting in their mendacious ways, do they? So please continue."

"I was only on the cell phone," she purred. "But he made me feel so *special*, you know?"

"For what he is charging you, he should be doing more than mere phone sex," said Toby, "such as giving your feet a tongue bath."

"That may be ever so nice, coming from you," she admitted, "if I was into that kind of thing, but I'm really not, being Catholic and saddled with all that heavy guilt that goes with the territory, as you so well know. But to continue with my story, If I may?"

"Do I have a choice?"

Tara airily waved her hand in dismissal. "Here comes the interesting part; he said that if I ever got on the stand, I would have the jury like putty in my hands. That got me thinking about what else I could have like putty in my soft, ambidextrous hands, you know?"

"You planning on taking up dry walling, by any chance? I used to do that right out of high school."

"What's the matter, Toby? I was only trying to make it interesting." She knew that he had spent the whole night on patrol, and regretted not asking him about it. But still, that didn't warrant his being that nasty to her, did it? Resisting a snappy comeback, she merely reached over and

131

gently kneaded his shoulder, not stopping even as she felt him stiffen and try to pull away.

"Nice Catholic girls like you just don't get it," said Toby, rather crossly. "All a red-blooded guy needs to make it supremely interesting indeed is for a nice, beautiful girl like you to just show up, preferably wearing only a smile."

Well, thought Tara, tapping the tabletop, *I guess I'm not the only Catholic not getting it today.* She looked away, and something caught her eye. "Don't look now, but I think that Asian-Indian guy seems to think he knows you. Don't pop the safety just yet, though. He looks quite harmless enough."

"Oh, no," said Toby wearily, "please, God! Not him again!"

Sure enough, the Indian guy started to head their way. "Officer Roland, good morning, sir!" His long wavy black hair was slicked back, and he wore a finely checked sports jacket over a black collar-less woolen tee. A pair of sharply creased olive-green trousers draped his long legs.

Tara noticed his two-toned brown shoes, a very nice touch, she thought. Tara guessed he was probably her age, or even a tad younger.

"Sorry to intrude like this," he said, smiling at Tara. "But I just had to thank Officer Roland again for the other day."

"Oh?" said Tara, shooting a pointed glance at Toby's discomfiture before looking at the stranger again. "That sounds so very interesting! Please do sit down and tell!" She beamed at the stranger, knowing fully well that Toby was furiously casting very sharp daggers at the back of her head.

"Are you sure? I really don't want to interrupt anything."

"Oh, you are most certainly not interrupting anything important at all," said Tara, patting the seat next to her. "In fact we were just about running out of any further pleasantries to say to each other, weren't we, Officer Roland?"

"Officer Roland nailed me doing ten over the speed limit on River Road," admitted the stranger, "and let me slide. That was a huge favor, you know?"

"Very interesting," said Tara, looking at Toby. "And just the other day Mayor McKenna was talking about the looming budget shortfall... Oh, well! I'm Tara."

"Venky, Venky Telluri. Pleased to meet you."

"So what do you do, Venky, Venky Telluri?"

"I'm a former AT&T Bell Laboratories guy."

"Ah," said Tara. "A former Lab Rat! Some of my best friends are former Lab Rats. Not that you would necessarily know them, since they all have been at Goldman for quite some time."

"Would you perhaps know Dr. Emanuel Derman," he asked with a raised eyebrow.

"*Eman*? Of course I know Eman," said Tara. "Everybody knows Eman. Mr. Quant. Worked for Dr. Fischer Black, of the Black Scholes option pricing model. Are you a rocket scientist like him?"

"Nah, I wish. I'm just a former telecom guy."

Tara laughed. "And I'm just a former investment banker, and Officer Roland is just a former Marine! We all are just simple folks, here! So what are you doing now, Mr. Telluri, former Bell Labs telecom guy?"

"One could say that I'm self unemployed," said Venky with a self-deprecating smile. "But I started a little dot-com along with my sister and a friend." Venky Telluri shrugged his eyebrows. "It's just a small three-person shop that we are running out of my condo. We are still in the development phase."

"That's fascinating," said Tara, genuinely. "Are you building a product, or developing a service? Or both?"

"You are very familiar with the dot-com space, I see," said Venky. "We are developing a product, and using that to build a service that we will offer."

"Give me your elevator pitch."

"Presence-aware, interactive, integrated, multimedia, in-termodal, messaging routed to suit your preferences at anytime, anywhere, to any medium, using any protocol."

"My highly trained, interactive, cognitive, multimedia, personal message receptors are signalling that the need for my presence is disintegrating very rapidly and standard al-pha-male protocol requires that I vacate my instantaneous spatial coordinates at this specific time," said Toby, rising to his feet. "Please proceed to reestablish this communications link at 1800 hours using intermodal digital service-discovery protocol."

"Roger that," Tara promised him. But for the present, she merely wanted to learn more about Venky's project.

જી જી જી જી જી

Slightly over an hour later, on her way home after her ser-endipitous meeting with Venky finally concluded, Tara's mind continued to boil over with excitement. Her impatience bubbled over at an old but neatly maintained Dodge

Dart that plodded along at twenty miles an hour, well below the posted speed limit of thirty, probably on a Sunday morning drive.

She downshifted to second gear and was fully prepared to catapult past the slowpoke when she glanced into the rearview mirror, and saw a Middletown trooper's patrol car right behind her. Immediately she shifted back up to third, and eased back on the throttle.

At the next intersection the Dodge turned right on red without fully coming to a stop, but the trooper stayed tight on her tail until she turned onto her driveway.

Had she had made a mistake in seeing Toby that morning, she wondered; she had come to a fork in her life, where two options lay in front of her; did she perhaps make the wrong turn? She felt guilty for even indulging herself to frame it as a question, for all of her upbringing screamed at her that it had been the absolute worst thing to do, no question whatsoever about it.

She had started to feel a bit of buyer's remorse regarding hiring Ramon, too. Must be something about the men in her life, she sighed to herself. She acknowledged to herself that it had been a mistake turning to Ramon; it had been a bigger mistake, she realized with a start, to have stirred the pot at Trundle, Morgan.

But Tara had a hunch that she was only too justified in her cynicism. Trundle, Morgan could have easily dealt her in, but only if they had chosen to accommodate her; but obviously they had other plans, which did not include her. It bothered her that they had chosen to not let her down gracefully, but had instead elected to unceremoniously dump her at the figurative curbside.

Her chat with Ramon that morning proved that her cynicism was well warranted. What had transpired was that despite his strong exhortations and urging, Mulholland had just as strongly declined an excellent opportunity to reconsider his position, lacking as it was in its foundation. At that point her two options were to forge ahead and sue them, or to quietly drop the whole matter and go on her merry way.

"You might as well sue for punitive and compensatory damages," he had said, almost reading her thoughts. "If you are going after money, then I can offer you two options; you can pay my fees out-of-pocket, and you get to keep all of the money you collect; or I can take you on a contingency basis sp that when you win, I get a third, gross of my fees and expenses. If you lose, you walk away and I eat all of the expenses incurred."

Were all of her problems due to the swath of wild impetuousness that she knew fully well ran deep in her veins?

She had no choice now other than to critically dissect a string of questionable decisions, setting aside her failed marriage for the moment, that she had made over the fairly recent past.

An especially haunting mistake was at Goldman, Sachs when she tendered her resignation a turbulent, heart-wrenching week after 9/11. Understandably, she had based her decision on the primal instinct of self-preservation, although her concern was not for herself, but for Jamie.

Months later, when she saw pictures of bright young American men and women eagerly signing up for the military, selflessly volunteering to put themselves in harm's way to defend her country, she realized that she, a soldier's daughter, had turned tail and fled the bloody battlefield at the opening salvos of what had appeared to be Armageddon.

In her mind, there was no recovery from a mistake like that; there was no way to crawl back to colleagues whom she had summarily abandoned, and try to meld back in as if nothing had happened, no matter how valid her reasons had been for succumbing to panic.

Her divorce had only added to her bone-deep feeling of worthlessness, even though she owned the sole responsibility of letting herself be swept off her feet by an irresistible cad, ignoring her mother's disapprovals. She now had a young daughter who needed her as a full-time mother, she acknowledged to herself, as did every child on the planet; and it wasn't as if she really needed a job to keep the bills paid.

A year after Jamie's birth, she had returned to Wall Street to continue her fulfilling work, albeit with many regrets at leaving her toddler in the hands of a teenager hired expressly as a surrogate. The unforeseen discovery that those surrogate duties had somehow been extended, obviously without Tara's knowledge and consent, to embrace extra-marital sex profoundly disturbed her.

Now, on top of the major distractions that she had heaped upon herself, she felt herself inexorably drawn to Venky's project. She had to admit to herself that he seemed to be a different kind of entrepreneur than the ones that she had encountered, both in the Wharton business school and while at Goldman, Sachs. He had seemed neither cocky nor desperate, but very balanced.

She recalled that a dimple had danced in his cheek as he spoke of the thing that he was building, that he called the

Chatterbox. In its simplest mode, he had said, the Chatter-Box was like a chat room. People could log in, and either start a new chat session or join an existing chat session. But that was not quite extraordinary, she had thought. Who would pay for something that they could obtain for free?

But in its most capable mode, Venky had explained, the ChatterBox was a fully blown out multimedia, multi-application digital telecommunications switch that was based on Internet Protocol, IP for short. It behaved like what was commonly known as a Software Switch, used to route voice-over-internet calls. All of that meant nothing to her, but she had sensed that Venky was extremely competent in all of the technologies whose buzzwords sounded so alien to her.

From the perspective of an investment banker, what mattered most was that Venky knew exactly what he was talking about; that was the very necessary ingredient. An entire operating company could easily be built around Venky and his whimsically named product; that part was routine. The unanswered and critical question in her mind was how the company would make money? The unanswered and equally critical question in Venky's mind was who would invest in his idea?

Isabella was at the kitchen table, reading a local newspaper as Tara slipped into the house. Jamie was eating a bowl of leftover chicken noodle soup, remnants of the prior night's dinner. Isabella had shrewdly added chunks of precooked chicken, from a can, to the liquid, and Jamie had not noticed it until Tara made the mistake of asking her if it was delicious.

"I don't like canned chicken meat," she replied in between spoonfuls of just noodles, pointedly dropping a large, pale piece of chicken onto the table, right next to slivers of carrots. Jamie ate only raw carrots, never any that were cooked; and she steadfastly refused to eat celery. Only onions that were minced to be unnoticeable passed her lips, but she loved noodles in any way, shape or form, sometimes even going so far as to nibble on raw, uncooked strands straight out of the box.

With a paper napkin, Isabella hastily swabbed at a thin trail that threatened to run off the table. "You were happily eating it all along!" she said crossly, but to no avail. The battle was lost, and they knew it, only too well. There were other things in the refrigerator that Isabella could have offered to Jamie, but she was not one to let food go to waste.

Isabella did not ask her where she had been the whole morning, and Tara did not volunteer any information.

Later that evening, she did call Toby, and in their own way they kissed and made up, albeit over the phone.

Somewhat reluctantly, Toby fingered Ramon as the attorney behind a series of controversial land-grabs by a local real estate development firm.

All of the cases had invoked a privilege called eminent domain, whereby a local government could force a landowner to sell the land to the government, so that it could be used for civic causes, such as building a hospital or a school. But what made those cases controversial was that the land was being confiscated and turned over to developers building condos and office parks.

So was Ramon some sort of a consigliore to an underworld crime boss, Tara wanted to know. Nothing of that sort, Toby assured her; family members of Ramon's wife were the developers, and they were of great wealth. It also appeared that Ramon DiCastro was most certainly not Italian, but was originally of Puerto Rican ancestry.

If Ramon's in-laws were that wealthy, she wondered to herself, what had made him take on her case? Surely it could not have been the money, although he was obviously not scrimping on his fees! Great wealth wielded great power, she knew; but exactly what was his angle? For that, Toby had no answer.

Dumpster Divin'

11:15 a.m., Thursday, February 28, 2002. Red Bank.

"NOW JUST WHO DO YOU THINK YOU REALLY ARE?" Jack Mulholland's menacing growl thundered over the phone, instantly commanding her total attention. Even though he had not announced his identity, she knew it was him. The boom of his voice was not diminished even the slightest by the tinny earpiece of the phone, and caused her eyes to bug out and her jaw to drop.

Instinctively, Tara pulled over the Porsche, rather abruptly and to the annoyance of another car behind her. Her fingers, tautly clutching the steering wheel, were starkly white and absent sensation as she feverishly cranked her head to check all around her, to make sure that he was indeed really just on the phone, and was not standing outside her car, bracing to rip off the doors to the car and then her head in short order.

Thankfully, no one seemed to be around, but her sole concern was her immediate and continued safety; what if he were to track her down? Then what? Would her dogs, protective though they were, be of any match for this beast? She knew beyond a shred of doubt that even if she had a loaded and cocked gun in her hand, with the safety off, she would be powerless to defend herself and squeeze the trigger. Nobody, but nobody, had spoken to her in that manner, ever.

Tara was shocked that it was Jack Mulholland who had uttered those words, he who had fought in Vietnam along-side her father and he who had worked alongside her father at Trundle, Morgan. Would Mulholland have even dared to think about speaking in those terms in the presence of her father, she wondered; what kind of a man was Mulholland, that he would speak in that tone to a dignified young mother, let alone someone young enough to be his own daughter?

"Excuse me?" she somehow managed to reply, much to her own surprise at being able to stay calm under the wither-ing ferocity of the totally unexpected attack. Mustering an unperturbed tone, she continued, "I'm on a cell phone, and the connection doesn't appear to be good."

"Stop that nonsense! That's the oldest stall in the world! I just got off a call from your shyster attorney."

Her relief was instantaneous; so it was not at her that Mul-holland's wrath was directed, but at Ramon! Still glanc-ing around to reaffirm that he was still not standing right outside, she interrupted him in a perfectly flat tone, deliberately stripped clean of any emotions that could be construed by him as a threat. "Mr. Mulholland, surely we can do without the profanity, can we not?"

Her words were not met by another onslaught, and she heard only his heavy breathing on the other end of the line. Realizing it was still a very dangerous situation, she waited for a few seconds, and continued in the same tone, "Mr. Mulholland, please go on."

She heard a deep intake, and Mulholland said "Alright. I just got off the call from Ramon, your attorney. He said that I ought to pay you $3 million."

So that was the thorn in his paw. But his reaction seemed strangely disproportionate, compared to the slights or even transgressions that he seemed to perceive, and that still kept her fearful. There had to be some other factor that could explain his bizarre outburst, she thought, but no explanations popped into her mind.

Tara forced out a laugh, knowing that it probably sounded very fake. "And you probably replied that you really ought to smack him on the head and throw him out the window, right? Because that's what I would have done, if someone called me with a demand like that! I don't blame you for your reactions."

Unexpectedly, Mulholland chuckled in agreement. "You are very perceptive! So what do you have to say for yourself, Ms. Morgan?"

"Good morning, how are you?"

"Let's not push it. What are you doing now? Can you come over to my office at noon? We can have some lunch brought in."

His office, and thankfully not some secluded rest area on the New Jersey Turnpike, after dark. To her, it meant that there would be other office workers within earshot, so at least he would not rip out her throat without the certain risk of being caught with bloodied hands. "Of course, Mr. Mulholland. That will be very nice."

"As you can understand, Ms. Morgan, the invitation is not extended to your counsel."

That restriction unnerved her very much, but it did seem to her that his presence might antagonize Mulholland again, so she resigned herself to go alone. "I understand. See you at noon, Mr. Mulholland."

"Fresh Lobster salad sound good?"

"That sounds good."

She hung up the phone, and just sat there, shaking.

12:30 p.m., Thursday, February 28, 2002. Red Bank.

A decade and a half earlier, her father had died in that building, of a single self-inflicted gunshot to his head. Maybe that somber thought was causing Tara's discomfort as she sat across from Mulholland in his office at Trundle, Morgan, forking what would normally have been quite a remarkable salad made with lobster, diced ripe mangoes, cream, lime and honey, served over a bed of early spring greens.

Mulholland cocked his head to one side. "Exactly what is your basis for that ridiculous $3 million, anyway?"

Tara had pondered exactly why Ramon had picked that number, in addition to her own question as to why he had even offered to settle for a certain amount, without discussing it with her. Ramon should have called her and made her clearly aware of his intentions, since she had surmised that he was only to act on her behalf.

She never knew what dreams her father had about her own future, but her dream, one destined forever only to remain so, had always been to work there for her father. She had spent many nights tossing and turning, wondering if she was even capable of working at Trundle, Morgan knowing that her father's death probably left a lot of their clients in the lurch, especially when the financial markets had tanked on Black Monday.

Everyone had to have experienced incredible difficulties in understanding her father's trading positions during the stock market's free-fall, and in piecing together whatever remained of his clients' wealth. On top of that, there had to be intense scrutiny from the Wall Street Journal, the Securities and Exchange Commission, the Monmouth County District Attorney's office, the local police, irate clients and so on.

Did she have the fortitude to overcome all of that? Even if she started working there, how would the other employees treat her, knowing the baggage of her family's history? Was this really the logical end of her impossible dream?

"I would prefer to leave a settlement as my last option," she said.

"The clause that you raised is quite valid," he smiled ruefully. "However, the reason that your father put that in was to prevent unqualified ne'er-do-well trust fund brats from joining the company simply because their daddy was a partner, or employee. He just didn't want that. You are trying to strong-arm your way into this firm based on a very erroneous interpretation of that clause. I have no desire to allow you to blackmail me, either." Mulholland looked back at Tara. "I deeply respected your father, and would dearly love to help his daughter out, but my hands are tied. I cannot offer you a job at Trundle Morgan."

Their venture capital business had collapsed, he said, and they had incurred substantial loss of their own capital that had been invested in a variety of businesses that had appeared to be surefire wins a scant 12 months ago. His economic outlook of the new post 911, post dot-com world, was very grim. By the end of the year, he said, their primary business was no longer going to be investment banking, but online trading.

Tara managed to keep the film forming in her eyes from becoming noticeable. There was no doubt in her mind that he knew that she would have no recourse other than to sue his firm. But she had lived through many business negotiations to appreciate that in reality the situation was far more complex than that.

Underneath his fit build, Mulholland looked scarcely five years, if that, from retirement. She expected his in-house legal department to be well funded, well staffed, and not really that overworked. They would fight the case well, with tenacity.

She would solely be reliant on Ramon, who was just a local real estate attorney, to work on her case for the next five years. He would drain her dry with his monthly fees.

By the time they got around to debating the basis of why her father had inserted that clause, and dragged out the circumstances of her father's demise, it would be at least seven or eight years before the jury got to cast their popularity vote.

If Trundle, Morgan won, she would lose. Even if she won, she would still lose because she would have to get some other job to keep her going until then. In any event, Mulholland would be long retired by then. So in the end, it was all a big chess game, with real people, that was skewed against her.

"Very well, then," Tara said, rising to her feet. "Thanks for lunch." She knew that this was the hard end of a long, tortuous road that had started in a battle-bloodied rice paddy in Vietnam, but she also knew that by cutting the lunch short, she was signaling her displeasure to Mulholland.

Mulholland walked her to the door, and shook her hand, devoid of any expression in his grip or in his look.

⌘ ⌘ ⌘ ⌘ ⌘

At a half past six that evening, Toby and Tara walked hand in hand to the Broadway Grill in Red Bank, half a mile away from his boat. She had called him, partly out of a need to put Trundle, Morgan behind her, but mostly out of a need for adult company.

Toby quickly glanced around the restaurant, nodding to the wait staff, who evidently knew him well. A waitress quickly dropped off a couple of menus on their table and lit a small candle.

Cupping his hands around Tara's, he raised his eyebrows and leaned in close. "Around the middle of November 2001, I overheard a conversation between two young women in this restaurant, " he said. "Here I was, dressed in civvies, waiting for a buddy from the station to join me, and these two hip chicks were at the next table, gushing over a couple of great shopping forays. Girl, you will never believe what I got, one chortled conspiratorially to the other between furtive sips of some coffee drink, and she did one of these maneuvers that you gals do so well!" Toby demonstrated that characteristic forward and backward paddle of the shoulders with a thrust of his upper chest.

"That was a pretty good imitation," admitted Tara, undoing a couple of buttons on her already tight cotton shirt. "But listen up RuPaul, you ain't got nuttin' on these puppies!"

She gamely stuck out her chest, but did quickly come to the realization that Toby's imitation was better than her scant version of reality. "Can you at least throw me a bone of a compliment before you go any further?" Tara asked, a bit miffed that she had failed to elicit even a whit of a response from him.

"About what?" Then came sudden realization. "Oh! Tara!"

"I'll let it pass, this time around. So what was it? Tell me already! You've kept me hanging for a while here!" "So what were they talking about? A boob-job? Should I get one?"

Toby's eyes lit up. "That's what I thought! So naturally my eyes bugged a couple of sizes larger, and I nonchalantly cranked my head and leaned in so as to not miss a single word being exchanged between these two attractive wenches, both in their late twenties."

Tara pouted that he appeared to have summarily brushed off her last question, which would have had him catapulting over the table during their fish dinner on the eve of Valentine's Day. But now it was probably received as a personal whine.

"Well," he said, "the object being brought to light, alas, turned out to be her great gold-hued winter coat that had draped some graceful creature from the animal kingdom in its past. Then her buddy shrieks *No way*! So the first gal bobs up and down like this," Toby demonstrated, again very realistically, "and closes her eyes, her eyes clasped in front of her, and shrieks back *Yes way! Genuine Shearling!* followed by an emphatic raising of the brows, and a couple of quick nods."

"That's it? All that oversexed titillations just over some lousy Shearling coat? No boob-jobs, no nipple rings, no Brazilian Waxes, nothin'? Where did all the man-excitin' things in this world wander off to?" mocked Tara.

"Only the very finest virgin Shearling for these chicks, my dear!" Toby asserted. That dramatic little term of endearment did not escape Tara, especially as it was the first time he had ever said anything like that. "Definitely a very nice find indeed, maybe from that store across the street, *New York Trends*, I had mused," Toby said. "Could it even perhaps be from Red Bank's very own pinnacle of glamour, fashion, style, silicone and glitz where Daddy's credit card is always, oh always ever so welcome, *Coco Pari*?"

"You certainly muse well, and with good taste to boot," agreed Tara, but she was mildly disturbed to hear him talk of other women to her, strangers though the others may have indeed been, but of that she really had no assurance.

"Sure you are not a closet cross-dresser?" She squinted her eyes at him, trying to picture him in a blonde wig and lipstick, but to no avail; his five o'clock shadow was too strong, as were his straight facial lines.

"So the proud owner of the Shearling continues *Yup, Middletown Train Station!*"

"Middletown Train Station?" protested Tara. "That's in the middle of nowhere! What did she do, heist some weary commuter at gun point?"

"To cut to the chase, according to the continuing conversation, apparently this coveted object was purloined one dark night from the Goodwill or Salvation Army bin or some clothing drop-off of the same ilk at the Middletown train station. The Middletown Train Station, for crying out loud! And from the charity bin to boot!" laughed Toby. "I should have pulled out my badge and scared the living daylights out of them!"

"But why would someone drop off an expensive Shearling coat at the Goodwill bin?" asked Tara. Then it hit her. Could it have belonged to some poor young woman who had lost her life on September 11? She could just imagine a grief-stricken mother or husband keeping a few items and dropping off most of her clothing at the Goodwill, instead of putting them up for sale at a consignment shop.

155

"Makes sense, doesn't it? I suspect that's what happened. The old Dumpster Diving Trick, yes indeed!"

"Here I thought you were going to cheer me up, and all you do is spin a tale to depress me even further. Tsk, tsk."

"Did y'all decide what you want?" asked their waitress, coming back.

At her bidding, Toby ordered first. A bowl of French Onion soup, and a Mushroom Swiss burger, no pink please.

Tara had not even opened her menu. "I need chocolate. Lots of it. Just bring it on in a spadeful."

"Got just your ticket!" smiled the waitress. "One Chocolate Decadence coming up. What would you like for dinner?"

"I'm going to start with that Chocolate Decadence," said Tara, and work my way back towards the soup course."

Running Naked in the Valley of Death

8:00 p.m., Thursday, March 28, 2002. Middletown.

As usual, Tara had a quiet dinner at home with Jamie and Isabella, and afterwards Tara went on a walk in the dark, taking only one of the dogs, Caesar, along. She had anticipated to be away no more than fifteen minutes, and the real purpose of the walk was to speak freely and candidly with Toby, not in the normal school-girlish furtiveness with which she usually called him from home to avoid eavesdropping, but in a solemn, purposeful tone.

On many a restless night, she had pondered as to exactly whom she was trying to protect with her secretiveness, and from what, but could not honestly arrive at an answer that made complete sense. She was, after all, a divorced, unemployed mother on the cusp of turning the dreaded three-o, in a relationship with a younger man who would not live to see the end of his own third decade.

It was that last part which halted her from accepting Toby without any confines, and instead she felt ensnared in a halfhearted, tawdry affair that had to be shielded from everyone, including herself.

157

So it was with great trepidation that she waited for him to answer her call, which then turned into a bittersweet thrill when he did. His Hello cracked a hesitant smile, and then unexpectedly, mirabile dictu, his I am so glad that you called... I miss you... and I wish you were here... were just agonizing ecstasy. She could almost reach into the phone and stroke his face, his light stubble tickling the backs of her fingers, his clean, earthy smell flooding her tightly conflicted senses.

Was there any joy superior to really being deeply missed?

It was the sharp tug of Caesar's leash that brought her feet firmly back to the ground. Caesar, an Alsatian less than an year old, was purposely trained to guard her from human predators, and took his task quite seriously, refusing to be baited by the plentiful deer, cats, raccoons, groundhogs, rabbits, geese, ducks, owls, hawks, falcons, egrets, eagles, turkey vultures, pigeons, doves, warblers, thrushes, robins, woodpeckers, blue jays, cardinals, catbirds and humming-birds, but warily watched skunks, snakes, foxes and the very rare coyotes, all of which claimed Monmouth County as their natural habitat.

She had quickly learned to have him on a long leash, so that he could adjust his pace and stance to silently observe, orient, decide and act without hindering her pace. He kept other dogs, regardless of their size, at bay with a low growl, and she was most thankful for that. She carried in her pocket a small can of pepper spray, just in case he decided to take on something that could best him.

In the northwestern reaches of the state, black bears were beginning to become a common nuisance as their once secluded stomping ground were being encroached by freshly built human estates, suffering the same fate as the deer herds did a decade earlier in Middletown. But this time around, it was not some nocturnal creature of which he was complaining, but merely that she had stopped abruptly in her tracks, and he wanted to keep walking.

Tara mostly listened to Toby for well over an hour, flitting from one inconsequential topic to another without revealing the one that mattered most to her, lingering just to savor his voice, without really remembering exactly what they were discussing, but each additional minute making it that much harder to end the call in the manner that she had originally planned.

Tara broached Toby about accompanying her on Good Friday, the next day, to one of Christianity's most solemn and poignant observances, the Stations of the Cross, called Via Dolorosa in Latin, for Way of Sorrows, depicting the Passion, or final hours of Christ.

I am a Catholic too, you know, he said, curtly cutting her off as she started to talk about the intensity of the emotions that it invoked in her, and she apologized, realizing her insensitivity. He would never attend Stations of the Cross, he said in no uncertain terms, and she dropped that idea.

Along the path, solely illuminated by the waxing gibbous moon, she caught some seasonal fragrant whiff of nature, and it only served to increase her reluctant longing for him, sucking away all her self-control. Stoically fighting the tears that formed anyway, she somehow managed to bid him good night, her canine companion mournfully chiming in with his sympathies.

Kneeling down on her knees and holding Caesar tightly around his sturdy neck, she found warmth and faintly oily comfort in its rhythmic expansion and contraction, until he raised a paw in protest. Instead of more tears, she only felt the hollow dryness of despair, the same crushing despondency that she had experienced after her father's demise.

Immediately upon returning home, Tara roused both Jamie and Isabella, who were in their pajamas, freshly scrubbed and snuggled together in bed, their eyes growing heavy reading a book on dinosaurs. Jamie had a little band-aid on her thumb, and held it up in dramatic exclamation as Tara tried to nuzzle her. But Jamie turned away, complaining that she smelt funny, and that was not as in *ha ha* funny. She would certainly shower, Tara said, but first they all had to go out and get an Italian ice, mostly for 'medicinal' purposes. Isabella had a questioning look on her face, since it was an unusual impulse decision, but Tara did not say anything more than hustling them along.

They went out in the Range Rover, Isabella and Jamie each still in their pajamas arguably hidden under a light coat, not so much as to ward off the night's chill, but out of modesty in case they were to be unfortunate enough to be involved in an accident. Tara left them in the vehicle, its engine idling, while she went into the store and bought squeeze cups of vanilla ice cream for her mother and herself, and lemon ice for Jamie.

A small chunk of ice cream broke off and tumbled onto her woolen sweater, one that a nicely dressed man had admired earlier in the day at a grocery store. She had smiled and blurted out that by a curious coincidence, she had been thinking about her sweater at that very moment. Hopefully they are good thoughts, he had said while walking away. Tara was quite relieved that he had meant it purely as an innocent compliment, and that had cheered her up for the rest of the day.

She quickly picked the ice cream off her sweater and popped it into her mouth. It did not leave a stain, but she would have to swab at it with some cleaner at home.

Tara sat in the driver's seat with her back against the locked door, watching Jamie devour her dessert without any complaints about her thumb, no longer held in protective isolation, but now back with the fold. If only, Tara contemplated, all of life's problems could be solved so easily and quickly with the swift administration of a frozen dessert.

Isabella sat quietly in the passenger seat, looking out of the windshield in front of her. Unlike many of her childhood classmates who seemed to have very liberal mothers who acted more like non-judgmental dear friends, Tara had never had, nor even wanted, that kind of a relationship with her own mother.

Isabella had always made it crystal clear, without saying so in as many words, that her personal parenting style was anchored in strict, unemotional discipline and tough love and it was never in her job description to appease and placate Tara.

Dictatorial was how Tara had usually described the relationship as a teenager, and that adjective had somewhat softened to authoritative upon returning home after graduating college.

On the other hand, her relationship with her father, while alive, had been very warm and relaxed. Not that she had ever considered him as a pushover, but even the act of being reprimanded by him usually was an even, calm period of collaborative introspection, of course drawn out beyond Tara's attention span, but otherwise neither unpleasant nor fearful that was to be avoided at all costs.

Tara glanced briefly at Isabella, wondering whether she would ever be able to confide in her mother about her melancholies. But what if she somehow managed to do so? There was no reason whatsoever for Tara to expect anything better than mildly disguised rebuke.

Tara did wonder as to how much longer could she put off coming clean about her amorous affair with Toby to her mother, to Jamie, and to God? In the same vein, would she be able to look her mother in her eyes and speak deeply and candidly about her failed marriage, her failed career, and her shortcomings as a dedicated mother to Jamie? If so, how could she do it?

How could she tell her mother that the clock was inexorably ticking towards Good Friday, on which day the Catholic Church, stripped bare of all its ornaments, and its enticing bells temporarily silenced, would celebrate no Mass, for that was the day on which Jesus Christ had been crucified, but would only celebrate the sacraments of Penance, where she would have to confess to her adultery if she wanted to observe, as a Catholic in good standing, His rise from the dead on the holiest day in the Catholic Liturgical calendar, Easter Sunday?

Even more so, how could Tara tell her mother about the deepest, darkest secret, newly formed, that she had shared with no one, and one that conflicted with every fiber in her moral body? An idea that suddenly, right before dinner, had just popped into her head without any warning whatsoever, hitting her like a crackling bolt of intense summer lightning, and its sheer cheekiness had made her gasp, causing Jamie, sitting right next to her on the couch in a TV coma, to issue a snotty complaint. Tara had wanted desperately to have Toby's baby, out of wedlock.

In an instant, that thought had dissipated her melancholy cloud, and had even brought a few rays of hope and cheer. It was then that she had sadly come to acknowledge to herself that the affair with Toby had to be immediately ended, and that she would do it right after dinner.

But that had been a goal easier said than accomplished. How could she have turned her back on the one person in her life that took delight in her entirety, and not just the cherry-picked highlights? How could she have shunned the one person who made her feel like an alluring prize again? How could she now tell her mother that she had failed in her feeble resolve to become an honest woman again?

ↄ ↄ ↄ ↄ ↄ

3:00 p.m., Good Friday, March 29, 2002. Middletown.

For the fifth time, Tara had replayed the message that Venky Telluri had left on her cell phone well before she had awakened.

I am lost, and in trouble. Will you help me, please?

Tara was not quite sure as to how to respond, since he was not really a known friend. She had never thought of herself as a go-to person for troubled souls, but she could see right through his even voice and sense an ever so slight hint of despair, so she had promptly called him back and invited him over to her house for tea that afternoon, not in the least bit concerned that she really did not know him, other than the time spent at The Flaky Tart.

So as Tara sat across from Venky that afternoon, in the familiar comfort of the study that had been built for her father, she could have dealt with him in a multitude of ways. She could have haughtily questioned his audacity in

165

bothering her with his plea. She could have icily stated her disinterest in being put upon by a passing acquaintance. She could have made mincemeat of his dream, nay, a pipe-dream, to create that comically named ChatterBox. She could, if she had so chosen, have said absolutely nothing at all, and watched him squirm in discomfiture. But all that was not her style, so instead she smiled warmly at Venky and simply said, "It must be very difficult trying to build a company."

His long, shiny hair slicked back, smooth other than tiny curls at the back and sides, Venky sat with poise in a winged chair across from her father's erstwhile desk. In spite of his earlier message, he seemed calm and composed as he spoke, with a look of eager enthusiasm and anticipation that suggested that he truly anticipated walking out with his troubles fully on their way to being resolved.

To quote Alcoholics Anonymous, Venky said, the first step in trying to solve his problem had been to first admit that he had one. How true, Tara thought, remembering that those had been her exact sentiments about her erstwhile marriage. Without disrespecting God, he said with a self-deprecating smile, the second step was to accept that there was someone better qualified than himself to restore his sanity, and the third step was to place himself in the hands of that person. "We are not business people," he said, referring to himself and his team, "and I know our limits."

But one thing that he obviously did extremely well, Tara had already correctly surmised, was to translate abstract ideas and concepts into marketable products and services; that was indeed a rare trait, although arguably it was somewhat more common amongst the ranks of the elite engineers at AT&T Bell Laboratories, of which he was an alumnus, than the usual hoi polloi.

She listened, nodding in agreement, as he spoke crisply about his dreams, and of his categorization of Chatter-Box. It wasn't yet a complete product by any stretch of the imagination, he was careful to point out. He felt that calling it an advanced prototype was appropriate, and that ChatterBox was the equivalent of a big holiday pot of a mouth-watering heirloom recipe tomato sauce simmering to gastronomic perfection on a hissing back burner in Aunt Millie's country kitchen.

In order for ChatterBox to become a commercially viable product, he said, it had to be finished. Having saved up enough money, he had resigned from AT&T to devote all of his waking hours to the pursuit of building his dream. He had not worked alone, he said, having been fortunate enough to have his sister, Jaya, and a friend Siddhartha

167

Sharma write major portions of the software that made up ChatterBox, in exchange for a slice of the pie.

It was their intentions, he said, to follow in his footsteps and join his company to finish writing the software and to put together the technical infrastructure to make it available to more than two people at a time, and to sustain a viable business. Skilled workers had to be hired to keep the operation humming, salespeople to market it to potential customers, help desk workers to answer customers' questions, financial people to send out bills and receive payments, and so on.

Unless he was planning on giving it away for free, and paying for all the bills out of his own pocket, he said, somebody had to pay for all of that. The big questions were, what would it cost, and who had the propensity to pay to use it, he wondered aloud.

But the entire factory would have to be built first, Tara said, before a single paying customer could be served, and that begged the rhetorical question of who would help pay to build it in the first place?

"Have you ever seen the movie *Field of Dreams*?" Venky asked.

Yes, she had; who hadn't? If you build it, they will come. She always had difficulty relating to the relevance of movie themes or sports analogies in business situations, and quickly brushed off the comparison. But if somebody built a pigsty in Beverly Hills who would come? It had to be the right product, in the right place, at the right time, for the right price. She could see that ChatterBox was not just an idle pipe dream to Venky, and that he had taken the first step towards commitment by resigning from AT&T, to work solely on ChatterBox.

He had also secured a name for his company, which he named Avakai. She had no idea what it meant, and he would only say that it didn't signify anything in English, as far as he knew. Anyway, the Internet domain name Avakai. com had been available, and he had reserved it in his name. Among other shortcomings, he had not legally established a company yet, and was at a loss as to how to build a company.

Registering a company was the easiest part, Tara pointed out. It was successfully forming and operating the company that would be the difficult one, which would require, as he had already recognized, skills that would transcend his own. In order to even attempt to embark on that journey, he had to put together a superb team of accomplished executives, each with a successful track record, and therein lay the most difficult challenge. In order to become a stellar enterprise required a stellar team; a stellar team would only be attracted to a company with a stellar potential, with gobs of capital nicely lined up. The question before them was simply that of how to get there.

First and foremost, said Tara, Avakai.com needed an angel investor to pony up seed capital for a share of the company, and that would just get the ball rolling by providing a nominal sustenance to the engineers; this was the phase where the fledgling company would have to run naked, as fast as it could to get to the next stage. Then that investor had to be prepared to throw in an additional round of capital by summer, which would give Avakai.com enough time and money to solicit additional mezzanine funding, that would provide them with enough capital to operate for a year or two, and also prepare the company to attract star executives with fat Rolodexes, who could get the deals and the funds to propel Avakai.com to the global stage.

Venky gazed past her and out the French doors into the distance, not speaking at all for quite some time. While attending Graduate School at the University of Missouri, or Mizzou, as he called it, he recalled being enticed by a coed to see the movie *Fiddler on the Roof* at the International Student Center. Much to his amusement, he said, he was introduced to the concept of a Shadchen. She nodded, familiar with that Yiddish word for matchmaker, and although she distinctly recalled seeing the play on Broadway, she remembered nothing of it but only her father humming the song under his breath on the way home, much to Isabella's consternation.

"Did it have a happy ending?" she asked doubtfully, since few movies of that genre seemed to have one. But he could not recall its ending either.

But his point was that ChatterBox certainly needed a Shadchen to make the right introductions and connections with the right people, and a wedding planner, to pull everything together. It also needed someone to prime the pump with seed capital that had to be raised. In other words, he needed a rainmaker.

She had worked with many entrepreneurs, their heart truly set not on their work, but rather on the allure of a big pot of money that they believed awaited them on Wall Street, since that was their perception of their rightful divine destiny, didn't everyone know? None, including the lusty entrepreneurs, knew that they were unwittingly pursuing only fools gold, and that they were only too vain to take to heart those who raised that distinctly unpleasant possibility. The recent dot-com busts bore testimony to the failed business models, but who, other than the Chairman of the

Federal Reserve had wagged a finger and pointed out the patently ridiculous effusions of irrational exuberance? But Venky seemed to have his head screwed firmly onto his shoulders, Tara concluded.

The dot-com way had been to drum up a loud buzz, often quite divorced from reality, to attract investment banks that could pump up a story to ensnare investors with the siren call of an Initial Public Offering, or IPO, when the nascent firm became publicly traded on a stock exchange, and watch the stock plummet to rock bottom, and move on to the next sure thing.

The old-school way, to which Tara strongly subscribed, was to judiciously inject enough cash to allow the company to survive, and to grow on its own. Organic growth, as her business school professors had also called it, had also been her father's watchword.

Her fathers also was fond of saying the he always preferred to run naked, speaking figuratively of the light, quiet, nimble and unseen Vietnamese guerilla fighters who were unencumbered by noisy, slow, heavy armor. In more somber conversations, she heard him say take only as many bullets as you can carry, and don't forget to save the last one for yourself.

There was a slight commotion outside the room, and Jamie ran past the open door, shrieking excitedly at the top of her lungs, with Jason in fast, close pursuit. That also meant that his mother Tracey Avalon was in the house. Ensconced in the library, Tara had not heard the visitors arrive, and was starting to get annoyed at her mother for not announcing that.

Excusing herself, she was almost out of the library when Tracey burst into the doorway, stopping short with her lips forming a silent Oops upon catching sight of Venky. Tara deliberately pushed past Tracey, closed the door firmly behind them and whispered that she was in a business meeting, and that she had no idea as to when it would end.

"He's cute!" said Tracey over her shoulder with a broad, mischievous smile. "Is he the reason that I saw you go into the Confessional this morning?" As Tara stuck out her tongue at her, Tracey continued, "And you were in there such a long time, sister, tsk, tsk!"

As Tara went back into the library, the thought of Walter Avalon as an angel investor briefly crossed her mind, since he had ample wealth, and certainly a well-established history of parting with it, but she quickly dismissed it for a variety of reasons, the least of which was the dread of Tracey constantly meddling, as she was wont to do.

"Are the kids yours?" asked Venky, brushing off her apologies.

"Just my daughter," said Tara, suddenly reminded of her recent desire to have another baby, and wondered how her father could ever have conducted business in that library, with all the distractions.

She recalled that as a child, she was expressly forbidden from entering that room, since she had a fascination to rummage through all of the drawers in his desk. It wasn't the papers, most of them quite important, according to her father, but the little clips, seals, stamps and other quaint instruments of commerce that had captivated her as a child.

She also recalled once trying out all of the rubber stamps and crimps on a particular piece of paper, which elicited howls of anger from her father when he finally discovered it, with his daughter's handiwork all over.

The swivel chair that she now sat in had also fascinated her, and she also remembered whirling around in it at full speed, kicking off against the table to increase her velocity, until one time she lost her balance and fell right off, splitting her head on a credenza behind her. That time, her father had only rushed to her aid by slathering burning tincture of iodine on the bloody split, but did not rebuke her. It was a lesson well learned, he had hoped.

At that point, she had to forcefully will herself back to her guest, and his problems. Not only was there something appealing about that young, ambitious entrepreneur that tugged at her, but also she now had a very pressing incentive to help him and his sister.

Yes, as Tracey had noted with smug satisfaction, Tara had gone to Confessional that morning, where she had readily and freely stood witness against herself, openly admitting to her trysts with Toby, holding back only her desire to have his baby; after all, she had reasoned, it had only been an impetuous, girlish dream wrought in a moment of misplaced emotions, that she had quickly snubbed out.

Even though she had been granted a valid civil divorce, in the eyes of the Catholic Church she was still married to Todd Scott Preston; so by making love to Toby Roland, she had knowingly set out to commit the sin of adultery that was grave in its nature, ranking right up there with murdering and stealing, and she had committed it with full knowledge of the sin and its gravity, and she had sinned deliberately and willingly.

She had agreed with the Father Confessor, who had clearly pointed out that the mortal sin of adultery had destroyed the charity in her heart by violating one of the Ten Commandments, God's laws.

After taking into consideration her circumstances, which she had deliberately not offered as an excuse, which would not have been accepted anyway, but which the Father Confessor had skillfully extracted via his interrogation, and her own ability to comply, he had pronounced her penance, which was to provide charity to a family in need.

Right after that, she had attended one of the most heart-rending observances, the Stations of the Cross, which depicted the Passion of Jesus, or his final hours.

So that afternoon, her emotions pretty much all wrung out of her by the intensity of the day's observances and activities, slightly weak from having fasted all day, but freshly armed with a crystal clear conscience, Tara knew exactly what she was destined to do.

Taking a deep breath, and casting aside whatever shreds of sensibility were vainly still trying to apply the brakes, she said, "I would like to invest $100,000 into your venture."

"You can write a check for $100,000?" asked Venky, incredulous, "Just like that?"

"Not right away," said Tara. "But I can arrange it within a few weeks, if we can shake hands on it." She didn't tell him that she would have to put on her thinking cap, but she certainly had some ideas on exactly how to raise the money by herself.

But she would put up only half of that to start, subject to strict covenants, and provide the rest only if those covenants were completely satisfied. One such covenant was that she would be the Chief Executive Officer of the new company; another was that the product had to be fully working.

First, the company had to be established legally. Tara started up her laptop computer and navigated to the website of the State of New Jersey. Right on the home page was a link to register a new business. Venky watched over her shoulder as she reviewed a list of different types of business entity, and chose NJ Domestic Profit Corporation, and typed Avakai as its name. She confirmed on another option that it was a Corporation and paid a nominal fee using her personal debit card. A few seconds later, she printed out a confirmation form and showed it to Venky.

"Avakai Corporation seems a bit awkward to pronounce," she said, regretting not having caught it earlier. She went back to the site and searched around to see if she could change the name, but was not successful.

"Let's just create a new name Avakai Inc. and register it," she said. "It's not terribly expensive." This time around, she selected Inc. with Venky's approval, and this time they verified that the name was displayed as Avakai Inc. before paying for it. Then, she filled out the names of Venky, Jaya and Sid, and printed out the confirmation.

Stuffing all the papers into a large Manila envelope, she gave them to Venky, with instructions to present them to Ramon DiCastro, who would draw up the necessary papers of incorporation and obtain a Federal Identification Number for purposes of paying taxes.

She saw Venky to the door, and as he left, a small twinge of buyers' remorse did creep into her mind, but she firmly closed the door on it and went in search of Tracey Avalon and the kids.

ↄ ↄ ↄ ↄ ↄ

5:00 p.m., Tuesday, April 2, 2002. Sea Bright.

It would not be auspicious to properly discuss business on April Fool's Day, Venky had said, allegedly quoting his sister Jaya; so they had picked the day after. Seated at the dining table in the condo that Venky Telluri shared with his sister, Tara heard of a new malady, Indian Standard Time, and a time-honored antidote that did not seem to be quite effective. They were waiting for Siddhartha Sharma, who was already late by over an hour. Three slender laptop computers waited on the table, humming to themselves.

"Tchah, we deliberately ordered Sid to come here at four just to avoid wasting our time like this," said Jaya, rolling both her head and an outstretched palm with a circular motion. "Please take," said Jaya, motioning to the hot tea and milk, spiced with cardamom, cinnamon and cloves, and a platter of stuffed pastries that she called samosas.

"We have been feverishly trying to call him, but to no avail," Jaya said, rather redundantly, since Tara had been sitting right there while Venky was making the calls. "Why even bother to get a cell phone when you don't use it to pick up calls? But when he wants to get in touch right away, he will call five times rapid-fire! That is such nonsense!"

The tea was quite delicious, but the samosas, stuffed with potatoes, peas and coriander, had a definite sharp kick to them that Tara found to be pleasant but overpowering. She surreptitiously extracted an analgesic from her purse and chased it down with a sip of tea.

Unlike Venky, with whom Jaya shared distinctive and pleasing inherited features, her speech seemed laced with native colloquialisms. Tara's gaze kept returning to Jaya's unseasonable short-sleeved blouse, and leather flip-flops

179

that revealed manicured toes with bright red nail polish. The forced-air heater kept kicking in very frequently, keeping the temperature well above the norm, and Tara felt stifled in her woolen sweater.

"Why don't we just get started without him," Venky said with a hint of frustration, and launched into a well-paced discourse on ChatterBox without waiting for their concurrence.

Although she had heard most of it during her two meetings with Venky, Tara nevertheless found the refresher useful, especially since he demonstrated ChatterBox using the three laptops. This time around, he did not liberally weave technical lingo into his speech, and Tara could fully understand the nature of ChatterBox without getting overwhelmed. At the same time, she could sense that underneath the exterior, still somewhat crude due to its infancy, lay technical underpinnings that had required a lot of thoughtful ingenuity and perseverance.

The doorbell finally rang almost an hour later, after they had talked about its usefulness. As Sid Sharma walked into the room, Tara saw his eyes sweep right past her as he explained to no one in particular that he had been at work, and was under the impression that this was just a casual dinner. Judging by Venky's sheepish look, Tara realized that

Sid was being truthful, and she hoped that her presence would not be interpreted as a blind date!

Thankfully, Venky stepped forward and introduced her.

"Simply put, Tara is the only one in this room with the education, business acumen and the experience to help us achieve our dream."

They discussed her role, her expectations of their own role, and a strategy for their fledgling firm, which was entering what was called the Valley of Death, a term used by entrepreneurs to define a critical phase during the incubation of a high-tech startup, starting with the full-time commitment of its founding entrepreneurs, and ending with sustainable, positive cash flow.

By the end of the evening, it appeared that all were on board. Tara pulled out four identical sets of documents and gave one to each of them. "These are the legal papers that we need to sign to get this show on the road. You don't have to sign them right away, and you can certainly have your attorney go over them."

Tara then went over the individual sections, and explained the relevance of each, affixing her signature as she went along. The others, including Sid, complied, waiving their rights to have them reviewed by an attorney. One section specifically covered the transfer of their intellectual property rights to the new company. On that cold grey evening, Avakai Inc. was officially born with the four of them as investors, with Tara Morgan as its CEO and Venky as the Chief Technology Officer. Jaya and Sid would be the first software developers. Lastly, Ramon DiCastro had agreed to be its attorney.

ℰℬ ℰℬ ℰℬ ℰℬ ℰℬ

11:00 a.m., Sunday, April 14, 2002. Red Bank.

Avakai.com quickly found a new home in Red Bank, on the fifth floor of a building from the early 1900s. The realtor who managed the premises had given Venky, who had been charged with finding office space, a hard time since they were a brand-new startup without any financial track record, even though Red Bank was beginning to resemble the notorious Dead Bank of old, with many downtown vacancies that had remained empty for over a year. But miraculously, after Tara stepped into the picture, all of the realtor's objections seemed to evaporate into thin air, and he even waived rent for the first three months. What had caught their eye was that there were a row of offices lining a wall looking out onto the Navesink River, and a huge unencumbered open space that Venky pointed out would be ideal as a programmers' area.

Venky, Jaya and Sid had requested a particular religious ceremony to inaugurate their new firm. It was called a Muhurtham, Venky had explained, that was somewhat like Feng Shui; a Hindu Brahmin priest had to bless the journey that was about to be undertaken by Avakai and its founders. There were actually two ceremonies that had to be performed, clarified Jaya, one to bless the formation of the company itself, and then another, called Gruhap-ravesam, to bless its new abode, both of which could be done on the same day.

Whatever, Tara had said, as long as it did not involve any chicken feathers or shedding of blood.

She had shown up for the event, and was taken quite aback at the extent and festive intensity of the ceremony. Over two hundred guests, many of who were Indian, filled up all of the rooms. A set of speakers had been set up so that all of the people could hear the proceedings.

Word filtered in about her arrival, and someone escort-ed her into the Venky's new office where a Hindu priest, dressed in white robes, a little skimpy in Tara's opinion, was busy setting up in the center of the room where a little makeshift shrine had been constructed of flowers, banana leaves and halved coconuts. There was no furniture yet, and men and women, many with toddlers and babies, were either squatting on large multi-hued cotton runners thrown on the concrete floor or standing next to the white walls.

Tara was amazed that Venky and his team had assembled one weekend and cleaned up the interior as well as they could by themselves, scrubbing years of grime and benign neglect, without even telling her about it.

Garlands of mixed flowers adorned all of the doorways, and someone was passing out individual flowers to the women, who either thrust it into their hair, as did most of the Indians wearing saris, or pushed it into a buttonhole; another was randomly sprinkling rose-water out of a pink glass bottle.

All that was missing, Tara thought amusedly without being disrespectful, was a bearded lady, and the priest probably could pass muster as a mystic fortuneteller.

Venky introduced the priest as Shastry Garu, explaining that his name was Shastry, and that Garu denoted a respectful form of address. Without interrupting his work, Shastry Garu graciously explained that under ancient Vedic principles that could be traced back to the dawn of Indus civilization, an aspirant looking for success in just about any activity of his life was well advised to initiate that under auspicious conditions. As a Brahmin priest, it was up to the Shastry Garu to take into account the nature of the undertaking. Whether it was a marriage, moving into a new house, starting a new job, going to college, or having a baby, they match it with the astrological factors that bode well for the aspirant, given his geographical location and time.

Shastry Garu placed a small white table of camphor on a ceremonial silver spoon and lit it. As it burned with a sooty flame, someone questioned half-jokingly as to whether the fire alarm was turned off. The ceremonies, which took less than an hour in total, were conducted in Sanskrit, and even many of the Indians around her did not seem to speak it, which did not seem any different from Catholics who could not speak Latin.

Tara saw Jaya for the first time that morning as she handed her a plastic plate with an array of what turned out to be a mix of sweet and savory items. She could make out raisins, almonds, pistachios and peanuts. Tara timidly tried all of them, except those with peanuts, her senses trying to absorb the new smells, tastes and textures, none of which seemed unpleasant at all.

Her only criticism was that the sweets were too sugary, but not any more so than a cinnamon doughnut. That seemed to conclude the ceremony, as she saw many take leave of Venky by shaking his hand and offering their congratulations, as they did to Jaya and Sid, and lastly to herself.

Perhaps she should have named Venky the Chief Religious Officer, Tara thought to herself as she walked back to her car, and taken him to the casinos of Atlantic City instead, if he really could dial in his success. But all in all, she appreciated Venky's humility in recognizing that with all of his hard work, it was up to a benevolent Supreme Being to bring his endeavor to fruition. Unfortunately, it seemed to be applicable only to Hindus, and it just wasn't fair, Tara groused to herself, that Venky had the opportunity to determine, a priori, the best time for him to embark on just about any activity of his life, whereas she could not. But in any event, she decided to pursue her dream, even if it had to be based purely on a basal temperature charting instead of an astrological one.

જી જી જી જી જી

4:00 p.m., Sunday, April 14, 2002. Red Bank.

Lying nude on her back, Tara contentedly snuggled up to Toby and draped her legs over his body to raise her pelvis ever so slightly, to hold back his seed. Coquettishly, she had teased him excruciatingly, almost to the point of no return

186

before permitting him to gain access to her. She had never been accused of being a good sneak, and did not profess to be one; but listening to Toby's steady breathing, she had to congratulate herself on a job well done.

እን እን እን እን እን

10 a.m., Monday, April 15, 2002. Red Bank.

Tara sat across from Gregory E. Sherman in his nicely appointed office in Red Bank and slid her open briefcase on his desk as he read through a detailed list of inventory that she had compiled for him.

"You have excellent taste," he said, probably not realizing that she had been merely the recipient of the jewelry, gifts from her ex-husband, well appreciated at that time, but now merely evidences of his adulterous guilt. Sherman came well recommended by Toby as an internationally renowned jewelry appraiser. Alas, he could not help her in selling the pieces, since that was not one of his services, but he could recommend several reputable local companies that discretely handled estate sales, and he could provide her with bona fide appraisals that would help her to establish an acceptable price.

His schedule was very tight but he could have the appraisals ready in a week, he said, attributing it to the last day to file income taxes, and many people had been resorting to selling off jewelry to pay Uncle Sam his fair due. That certainly wasn't her case, since her taxes had already been paid up in full. With his help, she selected enough items to fetch her a little more than the $50,000 that she needed.

Since the jewelry had been documented for insurance purposes, he said, that was ample evidence that she was merely selling off personal property, and that there would be no income tax consequences. That possibility had crossed her mind, and she was glad that he clarified it for her.

Tara left Sherman's office feeling quite content that within the span of a fortnight, she had managed to find herself what promised to be a wildly exciting new job, secured a nice investment egg. Speaking of eggs, with just a little bit of luck, maybe she even had an itsy bitsy bun in her oven. Life, she decided, was definitely beginning to look rosy.

Versace Meets Volcom

4:00 p.m., Wednesday, May 1, 2002. Red Bank.

Tara was quite taken by surprise at the sheer beauty of the twenty-year old girl sitting across the table from her. Tzippora DiCastro's tight skin had the golden glow of a late summer's sunset. Her tightly curly hair was a dusky blonde, and framed her sharply chiseled face, cascading down to her shoulders as she pulled off a wool beanie.

A long and slender nose smoothly arced from her deep, smoldering amber eye to her wide, pouty lips laden with the insouciance of youth. Simply spectacular, thought Tara with more than a pang of envy, and glanced at the skimpy resume on the desk in front of her. Her grades had been quite mediocre, and the only remarkable thing was that she had spent a year studying Yiddish at the Ben-Gurion University of Negev, although without attaining a degree.

Zipper explained that Yiddish was the traditional language of the Ashkenazi and that since the Holocaust the number of Yiddish speakers seemed to have declined very sharply, for one reason or another.

Her mother Debora had been born and raised on a dusty Ashkenazi kibbutz in the rugged desert town of Beer-She-va, which the Israeli Defense Force had claimed in 1948. Life on the kibbutz had been tough, but Debora did not really know how very much so until she had arrived in the United States as a college student.

Tzipi, a diminutive form of Tzippora, as favored by her Jewish friends, and nicknamed Zipper for gentile consumption, had been a difficult, rebellious teen, and her freshman year at college had been marred by a series of increasingly troubling episodes, though their specific nature was not disclosed to Tara.

Tara had gathered all that not from Zipper, but from her father Ramon, with whom she had spoken in advance. Ramon had cautioned Tara not to expect much in the way of volunteered information, but he swore that his daughter was really fully capable of multi-syllabic speech, since he had overheard her cell phone calls to her friends.

"That's quite a tan that you picked up in Israel," Tara said.

Zipper's eyes were very patient, and her face impassive. "It's not really a tan. It's my natural pigmentation. But thank you, I guess."

Tara felt her cheeks reddening from mortification. How to recover? She had inferred incorrectly, with Ramon being so fair.

Tara tried hard not to look at Zipper, struggling to over-look her inescapable conclusion that Zipper was not a good candidate even for the lowly position of being her administrative assistant, a newly created position for which she was being interviewed. After all, it was not as if Tara needed somebody to translate instructions on how to nail mezuzahs, which are little scrolls of holy biblical passages, on all the doorposts. It was not as though Tara really needed an administrative assistant, and it was certainly not Tara who had chosen to create that new position; it was in fact Ramon's strong recommendation earlier that day as he had handed Tara an unsolicited but very welcome letter of commitment to invest $100,000 of his own money into Avakai.com. Leave it to a crafty lawyer, she had thought to herself, to throw in a stinker of an unwritten but otherwise unmistakably implicit quid pro quo.

"I am also an amateur writer," said Zipper.

Oh? Really? Prithee, do tell.

"I created a little blog, using a pseudonym," said Zipper, "that's like a Dear Blabby kind of column, where fake people 'write' in, pouring their hearts about their personal problems, and I conjure up some tongue-in-cheek pabulum." Then the unexpected happened; Zipper actually cracked a smile, which was cute, thought Tara. "It's so completely bogus." With that, Zipper reached into her well-worn leather carry bag and pulled out a few printed sheets of paper, and handed them to Tara.

PERSONAL MATTERS

By Mrs. Siam

"The only Baloney that we dish up here is D&W"

Mrs. Siam,

My family, all of my friends, my teachers at school, and even total strangers that I bump into tell me that I do not have even a shred of common sense. I am really not that helpless; I do know when to come in out of the rain! What can I do about it? Where do I start? Who do I turn to? Can the Visiting Nurse Service of New Jersey come and help me?

Signed - Bumbling in Beach Haven, NJ

Dear Bumbling in Beach Haven,

Well, sugar, I checked all of my major suppliers - Whole Foods, Target, Starbucks and Sickels. It appears that none of them have any more cans of common sense stocked on their shelves. I dove into the frozen aisles at Juanitos International Grocery in Red Bank and came up empty. Heck, even Prowns of Red Bank is all sold out. The closest thing that Mrs. Siam found was a few large cans of Stinkum Farts at Funk & Standard, but I don't suppose you need that.

So what's a gal like you to do? Well, sugar, it's like my mama always used to say; if you can't get it at the grocery store (they always charge you double anyway), then by golly jes' grow it in your own backyard. Yes, it's really not for rank beginners such as yourself, but you can git yo'self an ounce of common sense by carefully following me own mama's recipe. Remember, no substitutions:

Rule Number 1: Never, ever do anything that will hurt yourself. Yes, yes I know that the guys on MTV's Jackass seem to do it all the time, but, sugar, believe me, don't do it; it will really, really, really hurt.

Rule Number 2: Never, ever do anything that will hurt someone else. They will find out soon enough, get really mad, and knock your front teeth out. Just ask that jock who got his done a while ago in a Manhattan restaurant. It will do nothing for your looks, and moreover it makes you whistle when you speak.

Rule Number 3: Never, ever do anything that will destroy your own, or someone else's belongings. Mr.

Siam promises to use his last can of Whupass on the next dingbat who toilet-papers our house.

That's all there is to it, sugar! Now send me your next 5 paychecks, and we are even!

With heapin' spoonfuls of love,

Mrs. Siam

At least she could write, thought Tara, and develop a web site, both of which were useful skills, especially in a technology company.

"It's OK, I understand," said Zipper almost inaudibly, rising to her feet and gathering her bag, a slight drooping of her upper body the only visible sign of her disappointment.

"Wait, please don't go," said Tara, eking out a smile and impulsively reaching out to touch her arm in atonement for making her feel unwanted. "Please do sit down and stay for a bit longer. I would like you to meet some of my colleagues." Not letting go until Zipper followed her bidding, and showed no further intention of leaving, Tara hurried to summon Venky.

Why am I such a pushover for basket cases, she wondered, her gut suddenly rooting for the troubled young girl, even though she would most likely require a tremendous amount of mentoring, the time for which would have to come only out of Tara's calendar.

ය ය ය ය ය

"You have no choice," said Venky, after he and Jaya had finished interviewing Zipper. "You have to hire her."

Tara looked at him, incredulous that he would even utter such a statement. How could he have come to know about Ramon's little covenant, since she had not had the time to share it with the rest? It was not as if she was trying to cut a deal with Ramon behind their backs, but she had wanted to settle the Zipper issue first, independent of Ramon's offer to invest in the business. If they could not hire Zipper, then she would have to explain that to Ramon. Had Venky spoken to Ramon without her knowing about it? "What exactly do you mean by that, Venky?"

He leaned back in his chair, a big, happy smile on his face. "She's just so darned cute! You have to hire her, boss! If you don't, then I quit!"

"TCHAH! That does it!" said Jaya, angrily as she stormed out of Venky's office. "Just for once, Venky, can you do anything without thinking with your … your…. Arggghhh!"

Very nicely put, thought Tara. That about said it all. But Venky did not seem bothered by Jaya's outburst, and only looked at Tara with an exaggerated, wide-eyed boyish sincerity with which she was quite familiar, having seen it in her ex-husband too, and which she easily dismissed with a firm shake of her head.

"Don't mind Jaya, it's every brother's solemn duty to tease his sister," said Venky, sitting up crisply in his chair. He was about to speak when Jaya came back into the room.

"I heard that!" Jaya said to him, and turned toward Tara. "You don't know my brother. He very simply cannot resist the scent of a woman," said Jaya, shaking her head. "Besides, she does not even know how to program! She will just be more ornamentation, you know, and such a total waste of money."

"Ornamentation?"

"Standard technical term for non-programmers," said Venky, suppressing a smile. "But I did not bring her in, Tara did. All that I did was speak with her, and she seems quite sharp, and she looks cute to boot. What do you want me to say? Zipper showed me her blog and it's quite a professional web site. We can work with her, and she will be a good fit."

"Now I'm really confused," said Jaya. "What's Tara doing bringing in somebody to develop our website? Isn't that our job?"

Only then did it dawn on Tara that she had indeed made a colossal territorial blunder. Before she had a chance to say anything, her cell phone started ringing. It was Ramon, and she let it go to her voicemail. Zipper must have called him on her way home. He called back three times, and she ignored it.

"I've been here since eight, I haven't had dinner, and I have a lot of work to do before I go home, by midnight if I am lucky," said Jaya. "Will somebody please tell me why we interviewed her and why we are still talking about her?"

"I brought Zipper in for an interview," said Tara, "to see if she could help me out…"

"Help you out with exactly what?" interrupted Jaya. "It's not as if there aren't enough hours in the day for you, Tara! I don't see you working till midnight every day!"

"Stop that, sis!" said Venky. "Tara's money is footing our bills. She does not have to justify anything to you."

"I'm sorry for sounding ungrateful," Jaya sighed. "It's just that I seriously question the wisdom of bringing in some-body whose sole talent is to display the whale-tail of her thong on a job interview." She looked pointedly at Venky. "Did you notice if she had a pierced bellybutton too?"

It was just that there was a check for $100,000 stapled to that thong, thought Tara smugly.

෴ ෴ ෴ ෴ ෴

Thus Zipper DiCastro became employee #005, and the first and only one yet to receive a salary. As she broke the good news to Zipper, Tara toyed with the notion of suggesting a dress code, but wickedly decided against it, a smile on her face.

As a new shareholder, Ramon became employee #006, although he would be there in the capacity of in-house counsel, only as needed, and would continue his private legal practice.

Venky, Jaya and Sid, who no longer worked for AT&T, and now Zipper, needed health insurance, which Tara purchased through an independent broker recommended by Venky, overriding Ramon's plea to use one of his relatives who was in the business. As an unexpected bonus of that arrangement, the broker, whose name was Read Murphy, invested $50,000 of his personal money into Avakai, with absolutely no strings attached at all, as he said pointedly.

Knowing that Ramon was involved had dampened his enthusiasm quite a bit, but Venky was his friend, Read noted, and somebody had to make sure that Ramon played nicely. Eminent Domain, he reminded Tara, was all about confiscating someone's property and giving it to somebody else, and that was Ramon's livelihood.

ભ ભ ભ ભ ભ

9:00 a.m., Monday, May 13, 2002. Red Bank.

Tara really did not have the option of not working on Mother's Day, since one of her stipulations when writing the Articles of Formation for Avakai was that a business plan had to be in place by May 15th.

Although it had been Mother's Day, Tara had met Venky at the office on Sunday, after attending Church and having a nice brunch at home with Jamie and Isabella.

The tasks before them that warm Sunday were many, but interdependent; they needed a road-map of the features that would be built, and their scheduled delivery; they had to estimate the effort required to meet the schedules; they had to estimate who would be their customers; and finally, they had to estimate how much revenue they could realistically achieve, based on the features.

Working well together, Tara and Venky had managed to pull together a crisp, cogent presentation.

Even with all their planning on Sunday, Tara's first sobering realization had been that they would not be able to put together a version of ChatterBox, with all of the features that would be needed to attract paying customers, before the end of 2002, instead of the end of September as she had been led to believe.

It had been very disappointing to Tara that right out of the starting gate they were going to take twice as long as expected to reach their destination, but she pointed out that the slippage did not materially affect the rewards that awaited them. But even investors who liked risk rarely liked uncertainty, and Tara's revelation troubled Ramon more than anyone else at the Board meeting.

Read Murphy looked over the top of his reading glasses. "What's the source of this slippage?"

"By the end of September, we should have most of the core capabilities ready," Tara said. "But the accounting and billing features may not be available until the end of the year."

"If we cannot bill our customers, at least until early 2003," said Read, "then we should make our failure a virtue by telling our early adopters that for the first three months they will have the privilege of being part of our extended Beta testing process, and that they will have a chance to use ChatterBox for free and tell us how to improve the product. Why can't we do that?"

That was exactly the solution at which she and Venky had arrived on Sunday, but she was careful not to point that out. Instead, Tara smiled and said that Read's suggestion was a wonderful idea that should be adopted.

Finally, they had to formally establish a Board of Directors to oversee the activities of Avakai, and indeed was a specific requirement of its bylaws. The investors, she explained, would form the initial Board.

By an open vote, the newly formed Board acted to appoint Tara Rose Morgan as the Chairman of the Board. She specifically turned down offers to be called Chairwoman, for that seemed too contrived.

Even with the most meticulous preparation, there are always questions that are never anticipated, and Sid Sharma asked one right after she had gone over the company's cash position, "When are we getting our money?"

"What are you talking about?" asked Ramon, with a look of perplexion that matched her own. "Tara clearly confirmed that the money is in Avakai's corporate checking account, and she will be investing most of it in Treasury bonds until it becomes necessary to draw upon it." replied Ramon. "Were you asleep?"

"The three of you put up $225,000," said Sid, looking at Jaya for support, "when do Jaya, Venky and I collect on it?"

Tara felt like she was going to retch, and Read must have sensed it, for he said quickly, "Sid, all of us formed Avakai. You, Venky and Jaya contributed ChatterBox, your intellectual property, to the company. Tara, Ramon and I contributed $225,000 to the company. Avakai now owns all of ChatterBox, and the money. All of us, except poor Zipper here, jointly own Avakai, in different proportions."

"If that means that I will not be receiving a check, then we have a problem," said Sid.

"No," said Venky firmly. "It's exactly like I explained it to you many times, and apparently you didn't listen. We do not have a problem, but you certainly do." Venky did not explain himself, but Jaya chimed in that the gist of the problem was that Sid, anticipating a big payout, had taken delivery of an expensive Corvette convertible.

"Let's discuss this offline," said Read, pointing to Tara and Ramon.

"I can't believe that happened," said Read to Ramon, as the three of them met privately in her office shortly after the conclusion of the general meeting. "Was there anything in the stuff that they signed to lead him to work up such a dream about a payout?"

"I don't know," said Ramon, shrugging his shoulders. "I personally drew up all the papers. But it's all standard boilerplate," he said, without any discernible embarrassment whatsoever.

That left them with no other alternative than to sit down together and jointly review the papers, word by word, while Zipper was conscripted to run out to pick up lunch.

"The original, unamended documents refer to Tara's initial seed capital of $100,000," said Read, "and clearly state that her investment shall be used to pay for operating costs, excluding wages and other compensation for Venky, Jay, Sid and Tara herself."

She had written it that way, Tara said, pointing to other clauses that had to be taken into consideration, to make it unequivocally clear that the four of them were to collect no wages until the product was ready and there were customers providing revenue. There were certainly other arrangements that could have been struck, she continued, but this was what had been negotiated and approved by all four of them.

They then examined the two amendments, one for Read's investment and the other for Ramon's, and they too did not provide for any payouts.

"I think that Sid should just go enjoy his new Corvette and take his mind off any entitlements, at least until we land some customer contracts," said Read. "It should give him a clear incentive to get the product out sooner than later." Read thanked Tara for her due diligence, while pointedly ignoring Ramon.

There were a few other topics that Tara needed to discuss with them. One of them, as Tara had specified in the by-laws, called for the appointment of external Directors, and it was at that point that she dropped her bombshell, that the first such external Director should be Jack Mulholland.

Read was innocent of any knowledge about her prior discussions with Jack Mulholland, and Tara made no mention of them, deferring instead to Ramon, who started off by asking, "Why would you pick Mulholland, of all the people in the world?"

Tara had not picked Mulholland out of altruism, but out of pure practicality. He was the head of a regional investment bank that had its offices literally down the street from Avakai; he had stated that Trundle, Morgan was entering the realm of online trading, and Tara thought that ChatterBox could be a great tool for their customer service; lastly, he was very well respected in the financial community, and his acquiescence to be on the Board would definitely imprint an aura of respectability on Avakai.

To her surprise, Ramon agreed with her reasoning. He was at a loss, however, as to how to approach Mulholland with an offer, and they agreed to see if they could come up with a plan.

∽ ∽ ∽ ∽ ∽

6:30 p.m., Monday, May 13, 2002. Red Bank.

Tara's break came on her way home. While at a traffic light, she threw all caution to the wind, and dialed Mulholland's direct line at Trundle, Morgan. He picked it up in two pings, answering with a neutral Hello.

"I'm heading up a startup Internet-based communications firm," she said after introducing herself, "and I would like you to be on our Board of Directors."

They spoke for a few minutes, during which he asked a few questions, which seemed very insightful, about Avakai's prospects and its competitive environment.

His final answer was *No*. Not *No, thanks*, but just a curt *No*; then he hung up.

The Green Fairy

In spite of Memorial Day having started off quite foggy, Tara and Jamie had made sure to kick off the beach season at the private Ship Ahoy Beach Club, where her family had been members for over three decades. From the front balcony overlooking Ocean Avenue, a two-lane road that meandered down the Jersey Shore, they had watched the Memorial Day parade, awash in a sea of Veterans, firemen, police officers, boy scouts, girl scouts, and scores of various civic and charitable groups, all proudly waving American flags to a marching band that was uncharacteristically solemn, in deference to 9/11.

Fifteen miles to the north lay the great Verrazano Narrows suspension bridge; ten more miles away began the ravaged skyline of downtown Manhattan, now unimaginably stripped of its iconic Twin Towers of the World Trade Center. The lasting image seared into Tara's mind was that of the downtown on September 11 of 2001, spewing gruesome, thick grey plumes that drifted eastwards towards Long Island. On that day, a certain young bond trader at the prestigious financial trading firm of Cantor Fitzgerald

207

had probably taken a final, desperate look southward from his window office somewhere above the 100th floor of 1 World Trade Center, and seen all the way to Sandy Hook, and down to the Beach Club, where on the last Labor Day of his life on earth he had taken his youngest child, a toddler son, into the kiddy wading pool. They had played there, sharing casual pleasantries and squeals of unbridled delight with Tara and Jamie.

After the parade, they remained at the beach club until half-past two in the afternoon, when they made their way to her father's grave, where at precisely 3:00 p.m., they laid down an American flag, and stuck their two little red poppies in the ground next to it. She had remembered to bring along a small picnic blanket on which to sit, for that had in the past seemed to keep in check Jamie's natural inclination to run around and whine about going home. "Tell grandpa anything that you want him to know," she prodded. "Just claiming *I don't know* is not appropriate," she added as a warning.

To her credit, Jamie talked for quite a few minutes, mostly about the things she had done with her grandmother, while Tara eavesdropped in surprise, learning of many of them for the first time.

Tara had somewhat dreaded visiting the grave, not looking forward to sharing with her father all of the unsavory things going on in her life. *Not that you can't see everything I have been up to*, she admitted wryly, disturbing though that was.

Obviously she had no problem with God being a silent witness to her misadventures, so why would she be so embarrassed at her father witnessing them from his perch in Heaven, she wondered. Growing up, she had always felt guilty after pleasuring herself, not at God having to watch her writhe in delayed pleasure, but at the thought of her parents, or worse her friends, finding out about her weaknesses.

Tara knew that if she herself had been born a boy, she could not honestly state that she would have gone into the Services, but here she was, picking up her father's torch that he held once high, helping others after the Vietnam War. She left the graveside with a light heart, knowing that at least there was one thing that she could share with her departed father.

ย ย ย ย ย

6 p.m., Monday May 27 2002. Middletown, NJ.

"Mommy! Your cell phone is ringing!" Jamie, her smooth face creased with a dark frown, held it by the tip of its antenna, swinging it to and fro like a rat by its tail.

Tara felt her blood gush out on its cleansing path from her womb, the cradle of life, into the toilet bowl under her tight thighs, marking the dramatic end of a failed possibility that had began with another ovum. She crinkled her nose in protest against the sharply metallic, raw, primordial smell that emanated from within her, and rubbed her forehead in resigned disappointment.

"Not now, Jamie. I need my privacy."

Jamie stood in the doorway. "Are you having your period?"

"I think I am having a really swell tea party! What do you think?" snapped Tara.

"I think you are having your period," sniffed Jamie. "Come see me when you are not so beastly." She lobbed the phone, which went silent with the battery flying in one direction and the body in another, onto the teak floor and quietly padded away into the dark bedroom.

"Close the door, will you? I still need my privacy!" Tara pulled off a flurry of toilet paper and dabbed herself. "Ugghh!" A smear of crimson arced against her thumb. She heard the last of the clotted clumps plunk down into the water. A final dab in a futile attempt to wipe away the dry stickiness and she flushed the dark waters before getting up.

Next came a session with the bidet, her second attempt at cleansing herself of the impurity of nature's profound admission of failure at conceiving. After drying herself, she got up, almost losing her balance as she stepped on the cell phone, which started ringing again as soon as she snapped the battery back into its dock.

Without thinking, Tara answered it, and was rather unexpectedly but pleasantly rewarded with the sound of Zipper's voice impulsively volunteering to bring a large tub of chocolate ice cream for them to share, and a movie for Jamie, without even a hint about Tara's personal condition.

Reaching into the glass-encased shower stall and turning on the water, Tara heard Jamie on the other side of the closed bathroom door. "Are you taking a bath?"

Tara reluctantly opened the door, knowing where this was headed. "No, dear. I really am having my period. And when I am having a period, I cannot take a bath; I need to shower." Needing to be alone, but nevertheless painfully aware that the innocence of childhood lasts only for the briefest flicker of time, she said, "Why don't you take a bath by yourself in here while I shower? I may need to scrub a bit extra hard."

Jamie nodded animatedly, her primary objective easily attained, and rushed to turn on the meticulously polished brass faucets. Tara spread out the bath-mat for her and added a squirt of shampoo into the swirling waters as her daughter instantly went from fully dressed to being naked as a jaybird. "Mom, if only one drop of water remains on my head after I dry off, will my head be still wet?"

Soothed by the innocence of Jamie's thoughts, Tara ruffled the child's hair as she stood by her side, testing the water with her fingers, as Tara had trained her to do. "I am sorry I growled at you earlier."

"I don't like it when you yell at me," said Jamie over her shoulder as she scampered into the large claw-footed freestanding cast-iron tub, taking a couple of big, yellow natural sea sponges with her. Neither do I, thought Tara, as she stepped into the steamy semi-privacy of the shower to mourn her new loss.

ↁ ↁ ↁ ↁ ↁ

Zipper apparently wore her clothes almost as an after-thought. She had on a pair of white hip-hugger draw-pants. Her tight lime-green knit top ended a good four inches of toned flat above where her drawstring pants began. In the front, the subtlest hint of dark highlights framed the soft reaches of her lower belly, and Tara could see the pink threads of her thong immodestly trying to peek out at the sides.

Her cell phone was clipped into the waist, but facing in-wards so that the phone lay next to her skin, to prevent it from dragging her pants down. Her long, curly blonde hair was tied in a ponytail.

If Isabella was flustered by their guest's racy attire, she hid it extremely well behind what seemed to be a genuinely warm smile. To Tara, it seemed as though she had two sets of standards, one set achingly high just for her, and a very liberal one for everybody else.

Moreover, Isabella even readily offered to watch Jamie if Tara and Jamie wanted to go by themselves for a ladies night out on the town, something that she would have just as easily withheld if it had been Tracey instead.

This certainly was a night of unexpected surprises, thought Tara, some quite unwanted, and some quite welcome.

"Not fair! Today's a holiday, and I get to do stuff with you, Mommy, all day!" Jamie protested, dashing her hopes. "You are not going out! No. En, oh, No!"

"Relax," said Tara hurriedly, resigning herself to cooking dinner. "I am not going out. Zipper's brought a movie for you and ice cream for me." Besides, as it dawned on herself, there was precious little in her broad arsenal of party clothes that could even hold a candle to Zipper's outfit. Elegance, she could handily surpass; raw sexuality was an entirely lost battle. Now suddenly grateful, she asked, "What would you like for dinner, Jamie?"

☙ ☙ ☙ ☙ ☙

Careful, whatever you do, just don't open it around your mother, Zipper had admonished Tara under her breath, handing her a plain brown paper bag. How intriguing, marveled Tara to herself, whatever could it be? Hustling Zipper by her arm into the kitchen before peering inside, Tara only noticed a green bottle nestled next to the quart of chocolate ice cream, and pulled it out just enough to see that it was the contents and not the bottle that gave it an unusually deep green color. Still, it was only a bottle; whatever was the big deal, she wondered.

"Green Fairy," said Zipper, in a whisper, glancing behind her. "Ever have some?"

"Why are you whispering?" Tara whispered back before realizing her incongruity. "It's just booze, isn't it?" Tara then read the label *Le Tourment Vert*, The Green Torment. *Whatever*. There was even an elaborate manufacturer's seal of some sort over the small wooden cork, so Tara surmised it wasn't homemade moonshine, but had indeed been brewed in France.

"It's Absinthe," whispered Zipper with a sly smile, lowering her head to be level with Tara's. " I brought some back with me from Israel. It's been illegal here …", and twitching her nose proudly, said, " since 1915!" Snatching the bottle out of Tara's hand, she popped off the seal and removed the cork, holding it up for Tara to behold.

"Anise," said Tara immediately upon her first tentative sniff. Then, after a second sniff, much more at ease, "And fennel. And maybe even a hint of licorice?"

"Anise, yes. Fennel, yes." Zipper shook her head triumphantly. "Licorice, no. You'll never guess the most important one," and she paused before spitting out in a dramatic whisper, "Wormwood!"

"Wormwood?" said Tara. Didn't epicuriosity kill the cat?

"Regrettably, not even the slightest hint of a worm in it," said Zipper, clicking her tongue, to Tara's amusement. Pointing with her forefinger, "Quick, hide the evidence! Here comes your mother," she said.

Tara hurriedly stashed the bottle in one of the cabinets under the sink and opened the refrigerator to examine their slim options. Jamie's allergies to food made dining with guests a challenge that Tara normally avoided. Nuts of any kind, especially peanuts, were totally banned from their house, since even their smell could trigger an anaphylactic reaction. The use of all dairy, including milk with all of its derivatives such as cheese and yogurt, and eggs, had to be scrupulously monitored, since Jamie was allergic even to its touch.

On top of these foods that had to be shunned, Jamie had never picked up a liking for vegetables, not even a token one, so Tara had to resort to all sorts of skullduggery just to sneak some into her already meager diet.

Fortunately, Jamie had grown very fond of noodles, which made Tara's task a bit easier. Originally, she had used dried, instant Ramen noodles, a dozen packets for a dollar at the local grocery store, but lately had switched over to whole-grain, unsalted Soba noodles made from buckwheat, even though Isabella flatly pronounced them as quite inedible for human consumption and particularly so for her old-school palate, and would mostly pick around them.

Tara offered her a sweater in case it got too cool, but Zipper demurred.

While Zipper cooked the hearty, slow-cooking Soba noodles by themselves, Tara sliced skirt steak, which she carefully thawed just enough to be barely pliable, against the grain into small strips that would almost fall apart after cooking, so that they could eat their dinner using chopsticks.

Tossing them into a heavy anodized aluminum wok, she browned them in olive oil with freshly prepared crushed garlic, diced onions and grated ginger root. Then a handful of trimmed snow pea pods went in, of which Jamie would under duress nibble on one or two, if that many.

Once the noodles were cooked enough, Tara drained them and threw them in with the meat and vegetables, finishing up with a liberal sprinkling of chopped coriander and thinly sliced scallions, which Isabella did not relish, and a generous splash of soy sauce.

Tara felt bad that Isabella did not share in her taste for simple, wholesome cuisine, but she had to tend to Jamie's critical needs first. Moreover, it was not as if Isabella could not eat the foods that Tara prepared. She simply chose not to do so, and that disturbed Tara immensely.

ย ย ย ย ย

Surprisingly, Isabella ate almost everything in her bowl. Tara was nevertheless nonplussed, since she did not really know if she had made it any differently. Had the presence of company tempered Isabella's expectations? If it had indeed tasted good, why didn't she pass on a simple compliment?

Zipper had very eloquently expressed her silent appreciation in the way she first cradled the bowl, letting its heat warm her hands before lifting it to her lips, pausing to inhale its aroma, sipping the delicate broth with her eyes closed, and smiling contentedly afterwards.

After dinner, they retired to the family room, where Jamie did not want to watch the rest of her movie, and most decidedly did not want to go to bed either. Tara agreed to let her stay up for a while, but warned in an unmistakably clear voice that at the first signs of misbehavior, she would be sent upstairs to bed.

Zipper either had not spent much time in the company of young children or had a decidedly mischievous side, and

218

just as Tara turned around after admonishing Jamie, she blurted out, "So what is your favorite toy, Jamie?"

Jamie's face lit up like a Christmas tree, and she dragged out not just one, but two hula-hoops, which did not even rank amongst her top ten favorites, and handed one to Zipper before stepping into one. Even though they had just eaten, and getting a child re-energized that close to bedtime didn't appear to be a good idea, Tara nonetheless did not want to appear like a fussy wet blanket, and decided to let them at it until things got out of hand, ignoring Isabella's scowl.

Much to her credit, Zipper had a great rhythm going for her, and did not flag even after a five-minute stretch, one foot in front of the other, knees slightly bent, gently and methodically rocking back and forth, almost imperceptibly; Jamie, on the other hand, danced all over the room, ducking and weaving and bobbing, her little butt swiveling away furiously and sometimes erratically but never failing her, and neither took their eyes off the other. Tara glanced at Isabella, and was pleased to see that she too was enjoying the impromptu contest.

Zipper claimed that her cell phone finally did her in by snagging the hoop, but Tara had a hunch that she simply wanted to let Jamie win. Upon being told to get ready for bed, Jamie protested mightily, in rapid sequence, that they needed a redo, that she didn't even finish watching the rest of the movie, and that she was ready for dessert. Since a tub of rich, decadent chocolate ice cream awaited the adults, Tara relented, offering her the non-dairy Italian ice only, and that was it, no more stalling.

જી જી જી જી જી

"You don't smoke, do you? I need a light," said Zipper once the coast was clear, with Isabella and Jamie having retired for the night. Tara had already supplied two each of brandy snifters, dessert forks and sugar cubes. Zipper had poured a shot of the green absinthe into each of the snifters, and placed the forks on top, each one cradling a sugar cube doused with more absinthe.

"Not matches," said Zipper, shaking her head at the little booklet that Tara offered her. "They'll just spit out chemicals that'll ruin the taste. Don't you have a handy-dandy little lighter like most everyone else?"

For someone that had never even lit a cigarette, Tara proudly admitted to having an arsenal of fire starters: a random collection of Zippos, emblazoned with custom logos, that had invariably seemed to show up as Christmas gifts during her investment banking days; sundry disposable long-necked butane lighters; an antique all-weather flint and steel set that her father had used in his days as a Boy Scout and finally a restaurant-style crème brulee torch that was still in its blister pack, which Zipper chose as the instrument. The torch was tucked away on the top shelf of a cabinet, safely out of Jamie's reach, and as Zipper reached up to retrieve it, the hem of her blouse rose up, exposing a swath of taut belly, pierced by a gold ring from which swung a small gold ball at the end of a short platinum chain. Tara wondered if Isabella had noticed it before she urged them to go out. What if her mother caught both of them now stealthily preparing to quaff a magical green whimsically named elixir that had been forbidden since 1915?

As she brandished the lighter, her finger wickedly dancing on the trigger, over the sugar cubes now iridescently pale green, Zipper said, "this really is not going to get you into trouble, right?"

Tara shook her head quite dismissively, but also shrugged her shoulders with a knowing snicker. "Light it over the sink, just in case it fireballs," she said, turning on the water. "Should I turn the smoke and fire alarms off? Are you sure that this is legal? Wait, let's not even go there."

"You're such a drama queen," hissed Zipper, jabbing at the air with the lighter, "You might as well stop wasting that water, now that this thing doesn't even ignite!" Click, click, click she snapped the trigger, "I'd take this gimper and that fancy bio-toxic bubble it came in and try to get a re-fund, if I were you."

It just might ignite, if only the child-safe lock was held down, Tara pointed out.

The torch lit on the first click, and standing three feet away, Tara could feel the heat on her bare forearms. There was no fireball in their cards that night, and her initial fear that they were going to have a tough time putting the shine back on the forks was unwarranted, since Zipper only used the torch for a split second, and by itself the absinthe shed a very pale, tenuous flame.

Lacking copious heat, the sugar did not caramelize to a crisp brown as she had expected, but only seemed to melt away and drip down through the tines of the fork.

Zipper stirred the drinks and added a couple of ice cubes before handing a glass to her.

Tara feigned familiarity and nodded when Zipper asked if she didn't just love the taste of the wormwood, before finally figuring out that it had to be the slight bitterness, after excluding the signature tastes of anise and fennel.

Zipper stifled a laugh. "Do you know what your daughter asked me?" After dinner, Jamie had asked her what happens if there are no more animals on this planet and the last one just ate the carcass of the only other one? Then will we all have to become vegetarians? She had even sort of attempted to answer her own question, stating of course, we can eat ourselves, but that would be silly!

That's my Jamie, said Tara, also thanking Zipper for the ice cream and the absinthe, confiding that she had been having a period that was quite a fierce gusher, only to abruptly cut herself short as she caught a fleeting, surprised look on Zipper's face. "What's the matter?" Tara asked, "What did I do wrong?"

"Nothing," said Zipper, "nothing, really." But after a slight prodding from Tara, she admitted with some embarrassment that a menstruating woman was considered to be niddah, ritually impure, and could not mingle with other people for seven days. It was so according to the Book of Leviticus, the Third Book of Torah, she said as if to waive any personal responsibility.

Tara was somewhat familiar with that part of the Old Testament that had to do with general uncleanliness, and that spoke of a man who spilt his seed, and also spoke of a woman who 'hath her issue of blood'. "So what's such a

223

woman to do?" asked Tara. How would she feed her family, or hug a loved one?

"In my faith, the source of all purity is life itself. A woman's flow indicates the death of a potential life. We believe that a pregnancy fills the mother's life with purity and holiness, and when she misses that opportunity, she is considered niddah."

In her own case that evening, mused Tara, it had gone beyond simply missing an opportunity to have a pregnancy; it was the wretched, gruesome and quite unwelcome termination of one, and she turned away, feeling the tears well up in her eyes. "So women who are not pregnant are impure?" Tara asked, with her head bent down as she stacked the dishes into the dishwasher.

"Didn't imply that. The impurity refers to a spiritual state, not a physical one. But we have a ritual called a mikvah that takes care of that."

"That's the thing you nail on walls?" asked Tara.

"No, you're thinking of a mezuzah, or holy scroll, and it goes on a doorpost, not on a wall. A mikvah looks like a miniature pool, but it's really built to strict religious specifications. It's supposed to be filled with rainwater; now try doing that in the middle of the desert, and you take a dip in it."

"Somehow I don't see myself taking a dip in a pool after having a nasty period," said Tara. "I still don't get how it works."

"It's simple. Take my mom as an example. She gets a period, OK? From the time it starts, going on until seven days after its end, she is forbidden to have sex. Now that's a really horrible thought, my mom having sex! Anyway, on the night of the seventh day after the flow stops, she has to go take a dip in the mikvah. By then, she has had quite a few showers, so it's not like ... you know."

"So she goes to this public pool thing, takes a dip, gets out, showers and then trots on home to put a big smile on big daddy's face?" Tara had to laugh.

Zipper laughed. "It's probably straight from the dip to the smile. No shower necessary."

"Even after taking a dip in that public mickey?

"You don't even think about getting into that thing with even a lick of anything dirty," explained Zipper. "You walk in, and there's a big Helga to frisk you down. You can't even wear contacts in the mikvah. The only thing you are allowed to keep is your birthday suit, and Helga makes sure that even your toenails are clipped. Then, you shower, shampoo, scrub really well behind the ears, and then, and only then, are you allowed to go dip in the mikvah. Trust me, you can't sneak anything past these Helgas standing guard."

"So, coming back to the part about putting a big smile on big daddy's face; basically there's no hanky panky for two weeks every month? There must be a lot of makin' up for lost times, no?"

"That's exactly the point behind the mikvah," said Zipper. "A little bride gets to keep her guy on a very tight leash, since he is certainly not getting it for half the month. At least, not from her, anyway."

"So how come Mr. and Mrs. DiCastro did not end up with a Cheaper by the Dozen?"

Zipper sighed. "Truth is, I really don't think my parents have a great thing going."

"Oh, I'm sorry!" said Tara, quite embarrassed. "I was just being silly."

"Not your fault. I think they started drifting apart a long time ago. I mean, it's not like she throws rolling pins and stuff at Dad, but you can tell the milk has long curdled."

Tara wondered if that had anything to do with Zipper going away to Israel, but kept that thought to herself. The belly ring intrigued her, if only for the fact that in the Jewish faith body piercing, even for earrings, was considered mutilation, and hence forbidden. Somehow, that did seem anomalous with Zipper's deep knowledge and understanding of the Torah. Moreover, she had the vaguely disturbing feeling, based on Zipper's nonchalance, that there were probably more, generally unseen.

That seemed to take the buoyancy out of Zipper, and declining offers of another scoop of chocolate ice cream she took one for the road and left.

Sari, So Sari

6:00 p.m., Saturday, August 24, 2002. Sea Bright.

"You may want to take off your pantyhose," suggested Jaya, to Tara's astonishment.

"Oh? Why?"

Zipper snorted. "You really want to leave them on? I hate those things, and can't get them off soon enough."

They were gathered at the Telluri's residence in Sea Bright, to celebrate Venky's birthday. It had been Zipper's idea for them to dress like Jaya, in an Indian Sari, and Tara was quite reluctant at first, but allowed herself to be convinced by Zipper's enthusiasm.

Jaya shook her head from side to side. "The sari will cover you from the waist down to your feet, so there is really no need. I am not wearing any myself. Besides, back home in India it gets too hot for anything like that." She stuck her foot forward, and pulled up on her sari. A small permanently tanned, naked foot with tight skin, devoid of any veins, peeked out from underneath. An elaborate silver anklet with a myriad of tiny bells wrapped around her trim ankle. Glossy red nail polish on her toenails matched that on her fingertips.

"Jaya, you tramp! Do you have any anklets for us," asked Zipper.

Jaya walked lightly over to a dresser, the bells tinkling in a tight beat. Rummaging through one of the drawers of her dresser, she handed them each a pair of anklets. "These are not as noisy, and you don't have to wear them if you don't want to." She excused herself and left the room to answer the phone.

Tara nudged Zipper, pointing to a set of large bells, held together on a thick, padded red strap with a buckle. Zipper picked one up and jiggled them. "These are worn by temple dancers in India," she said, as if that should be self-evident. Not to be confused with courtesans, she said, although they were common in the Indian palaces of yore. Temple dancing was a traditional, classical form of Indian dance, Zipper said, called Bharata Natyam that celebrated the celestial dances of their gods. Tara wondered what Jaya did with them, since they were obviously too big and too noisy for general use, however romantic the situation.

"Didn't you notice the exaggerated way that Jaya walked over to the dresser?" As Tara shook her head in response, Zipper pointed to a few large portraits hanging on the wall, of Jaya in very elaborate traditional garb. "She is an accomplished Bharata Natyam dancer, and had her solo debut when she was sixteen."

Tara knew that Zipper and Jaya had established a warm relationship in spite of their rocky start, but was not aware that they had been spending time socializing outside work. "Have you decided about the pantyhose," said Jaya, coming back into her room.

"She is taking them off," said Zipper firmly, answering for her, having taken off her own thong and set it aside. "Underwear is optional, and not necessary at all, Tara. I mean, in India it is perfectly normal for women to go without western lingerie." So what did they wear underneath? Petticoats. No panty lines, ever.

"Well, if you put it that way," said Tara, musing to herself about the interesting direction that evening had taken.

"You probably should keep your bra on, though," said Jaya, wagging her finger. "After all, you don't want to give the boys any strange ideas." Tara knew that she used the word boys to denote young men, as was common in Indian dialog. Zipper was quite adamant about going native, and decided to dispense with her bra.

Tara slipped on a short white cotton petticoat that Jaya handed, one to her and the other to Zipper. The petticoat knotted as would pajama bottoms. "In India older women put on long petticoats, but the younger ones prefer these shorties," explained Jaya.

The blouses turned out to be mostly Spandex tops that Tara judged would barely, if at all, cover the bottom of her bra. Naturally, Zipper chose a sleeveless one with a deep vee neck that did little to hide the swell of her breasts, her cleavage and pink nipples, which were free of any adornment, much to Tara's surprise. "I defy anyone to see them through the sari," she said.

"For most functions I would never wear these," Jaya said shaking her head. She liked to wear them, but only for casual occasions. Most formal saris came with extra material to make a matching blouse, which had to be done by seamstresses, since women in India would not allow male tailors to measure them, although they did not seem to draw that line for obstetricians. If a male tailor was the only choice, the women would take the measurements themselves and jot them down on a piece of paper. "We most certainly would not want them to measure us, especially here, you know," Jaya motioned with both palms in front of her chest, her head bobbing from side to side. "So these days, it is simply very convenient to simply wear these Spandex tops. In fact, some of the more forward girls even wear strapless tank tops!"

"We normally wear silk or cotton saris. But silk is so hard to keep in place, especially if you have never worn a sari before," said Jaya. "So for now, cotton is best, you know?" She pulled out two saris. Tara gasped. One was a checked print of gold squares on a green background. The edge was covered with a salmon-colored band of about three inches, which had a shiny metallic weave. She reached out and stroked the band, which was actually made of thin gold fibers woven into the material, forming what was called a Zari.

The material was so light that Tara could almost see right through it as she slid her hand underneath the first fold. "And this is cotton?" she asked, unbelievingly.

"It is really cotton," insisted Jaya, smiling. "Let me show you the silk one here." She handed Tara a creamy white sari that weighed in at absolutely zero. It almost floated in Tara's grasp. It had a simple border of deer, drawn very simply in two dimensions, without any shading, and the center was taken up by a large but equally simple painting of a voluptuous young woman, with flowing hair and robes, embracing a deer. The lady depicted was Shakuntala, said Jaya. In Hindu mythology, a king named Dushyanta shot the deer with an arrow from his bow, not realizing that it was her pet.

"My lord! Did he kill it? I hope not!" exclaimed Tara, her eyes searching the sari for signs of blood on the deer. He did not, but she did end up marrying the king, and ended up bearing him a son who they named Bharata. It was after him that India was referred to locally as Bharat.

After a bit of heated negotiation, Zipper got to wear the Shakuntala sari, leaving Tara with the green and gold one, which she thought suited her complexion well. Jaya did most of the elaborate draping of the sari, which seemed mostly to be folding sections into wide vertical pleats that were tucked into the waistband of the petticoat, and continuing around the waist a couple of times, to have the final section, called the pallu, free to cross the chest from the right waist over onto the left shoulder, with the option to merely dangle from there, or to swing it back over the right shoulder in case it got too cold, said Jaya. Tara had a hunch that left to herself Zipper would have just left her chest free of the pallu, but draped it only to humor Jaya. She had also made sure that her petticoat was tied quite low on her hips, exposing her navel piercing. "In India it is quite common to display the belly button," said Jaya.

Jaya had a huge selection of jewelry, made of the traditional Indian 22-carat gold, with deep red rubies, green emeralds, blue sapphires and sparkling diamonds. She wore a set of diamond earrings, made of 6 glittering stones set in a rounded gold hexagon, with a seventh one in the center. Zipper chose an intricate necklace that had Nataraja, the Hindu God of Dance, as a pendant, craftily wearing it so that it lay on top of the light pallu, thereby accentuating her cleavage, as Tara noticed with some envy.

Tara studied herself in a full-length mirror, and was surprised to see that the sari draped her figure very well, due to the fine material and Jaya's skillful wrapping. Jaya had also recommended pinning the pallu to the blouse atop the left shoulder, "so that you don't have to constantly keep tending to it, but some cunning women let it fall on purpose just to tease the boys."

It took Tara a few steps to learn to walk while wearing the sari, which meant taking small, smooth, gliding steps, without raising the foot much, which also made the little bells on the anklets to gently chime *come hither*, thought Tara.

ⁿ ⁿ ⁿ ⁿ ⁿ

Tara surveyed the food, which smelt incredibly appetizing, but none of which she recognized, neatly arranged on a serving buffet table. She looked for the familiar Vindaloo, Tandoori, Korma, Daal and Rotis, but came up short. Zipper seemed to have no problem swiftly ladling everything, in different proportions, without any hesitation.

It was genuine homemade South Indian cuisine, said Venky, whom she was seeing for the first time that evening, and quite different from the North Indian dishes that were normally served in restaurants; for one, South Indians were mostly vegetarian, and did not use the strong masalas and curry powders favored up north. "Let me help you, if I may," he said. First, there were three different kinds of rice, all made of the basmati grains; yellow saffron rice with roasted lentils and fiery dried red peppers, white rice premixed with yogurt, chopped cilantro and some light seasonings, and of course plain white rice. Then there were small, whole elongated eggplants that had their green caps removed, and sliced lengthwise from opposite ends, each cut perpendicular to the other, stuffed with a mix of herbs and spices, and fried in ghee, which was clarified butter. There was something called pesara pappu, or steamed Mung beans.

There were a few small dishes that Venky passed over, saying that they would be just too spicy, whereas the rest of the food was prepared to be very mild, and she thanked him for that.

There were about a dozen guests, all of Indian origin; *Desis*, meaning from the country, except for Tara and Zipper. Everyone sat at a table which had all of its leaves put in, so there was adequate elbow room. "Sit next to me," said Zipper, sitting across from Venky. His birthday was on the 11th, but the plan was for most of the guests to stay up the whole night playing cards, for small wagers of money, eating Indian snacks and drinking Scotch whiskey. That was a very common pastime for Indians, said Jaya.

"Single malt Scotch," said Venky. "Nothing but the best for my *Desi* gambling buddies."

"Stay away from these card sharks, trust me," whispered Zipper, "they look so innocent but will clean their grandmother out with no remorse. Also, sister, you need to lose the silverware, and eat with your hands. It's easy. But first, did you wash your hands? With soap?"

"Yes," Tara lied.

Zipper gave her a skeptical look, but picked up a small clump of rice with just the pads of her four fingers; the right hand only, never the left, she admonished, scooping up a small dab of the lentils with the rice. Then using the pads of her fingers and the edge of her thumb, she effort-lessly rolled a small tight ball, with a fluidity that indicated prior experience. She offered the ball to Tara, placing her left hand well below, to catch any that dropped. "Open. Remember, do not touch my fingers with your tongue. The saliva of others is considered very unclean in India."

"Did you wash your hands," said Tara.

"Of course," said Zipper, bringing her fingers close to Tara's lower lip, and carefully pushing the rice ball in with the back of her thumb, "this morning, before I walked the dog, as a matter of fact." She flicked the remnants gently onto her plate. "And please don't lick your own fingers either."

"Could you please pass the pickles?" asked one of the guests.

Tara spotted a little silver dish with dark brown, smelly stuff that had been passed around, and reached for it.

"No, not the Magai, the Avakai, please."

"That dish right next to it," pointed out Zipper quickly. "The red one with the big chunks of green mango." She reached out with the tips of her fingers and nudged the dish towards Tara. "Whatever you do, do not try it! It's got a mighty potent zing to it that will stay with you for a couple of days!" Zipper theatrically fanned her palm in front of her mouth.

"Come on, it's really not that bad," protested Venky, "I mean, not after you put a dollop of yogurt or ghee."

"Ghee... what's that?" asked Tara, tongue in cheek. "That sounds like a nice name for a company." Then she caught sight of Zipper's smoldering eyes. "May I have some of the fried eggplant, please?"

എ എ എ എ എ

After dinner, Venky, directed Zipper and Tara to relax outside on the balcony while he and Jaya rang up an uncle in India, since the rest were getting a card game going on the dining table.

"I have to tell you a really funny story first about that uncle," said Jaya upon their return. "Two years ago, I went to India for three weeks. At my request my uncle prepared a new set of astrological charts for me, and as he was explaining it to me he mentioned that I would be getting a new car." Jaya waved a hand dismissively. "Tchah! I told him that there was simply no way that would happen, since I had just purchased a new Toyota Camry less then 11 months ago. So of course to be nice I said thank you and went on my merry way. Then from the airplane on my way back I called Venky on the air phone and reminded him to be at the airport to pick me up; you see, he is so very forgetting, and also I wanted to make sure he was not sleeping. Like most boys he tends to sleep all the time when there is no one to remind him that he must not sleep so much. When I remind him, he says why, akkaya, what harm is there in sleeping? Tchah!"

"Yes, I know!" agreed Tara. "He is so… forgetting!"

"When I called him on the phone he said not to worry, but my poor little Camry was totally damaged beyond repair."

"My goodness! What happened? Did Venky wreck it?"

"Not at all, the silly fool took it for a spin one night and left the sunroof wide open and forgot to even close it, and it rained all night long ruining the entire inside of the car so that everything became moldy and I had to pretty much throw the whole car away because the Toyota dealer said it will be too expensive to have it properly repaired and the car would never lose its bad smell. Tchah!"

"How about that! And your uncle astrologically predicted that it would happen! That is unbelievable!" Deep down, she wondered if it was perhaps occult or even something far worse.

"For me it is very believable because I always knew that astrology always comes true," said Jaya. "In fact, nothing gets done in India without first consulting the astrological charts." There were two types of astrological charts, Jaya explained; the Jataka charts, based on a person's birthday and birth time, which were used to forecast a person's future, and Muhurta charts to pick a very auspicious time to perform an event like a marriage or the naming of a baby. That was why they had performed a Muhurtam when they launched Avakai.com.

"Why don't you get your astrology done," said Zipper without a trace of mischief, as Tara looked at her strangely. "Venky did mine a few months ago, and he had correctly identified a few things that had happened in my life. All that I had to do was tell him my time, date and place of birth."

"I thought astrology only portended the future," Tara said.

"It predicts everything from the person's birth to his death," said Venky. "In cases where the person preparing the chart has no a priori knowledge of the person's real history, it can be used to test the astrologer's accuracy."

"For whatever it's worth, September 15, 1972. 12:34 a.m., Riverview Hospital in Red Bank," said Tara.

"Give me a few minutes," said Venky, going inside.

Venky arrived with a small sheaf of papers half an hour later. As he sat down, Tara said, "It would be a perfect night if the moon was above the ocean instead of being over the rooftops." August 22 had been a full moon, and there was only a slight nick of it missing. *Mommy, look. Someone took a chomp out of the moon*, Jamie had exclaimed a long time ago.

"If the moon was above the ocean right now," he said, "you would have a very different future." The seriousness in his tone scared her, and even Jaya looked askance at him. "You were born in Red Bank New Jersey on September 15, 1972 at 12:34 a.m."

Jaya laid a hand on Venky's arm. "Before you begin, when was Daylight Savings implemented in New Jersey?" She explained that until 1966, there was no federal law concerning Daylight Savings. So every state could set its own policies of when it started and ended, and in fact many did exactly that!

Spring forward and fall backward had come to Tara's mind, and nothing else, and it bothered her that Jaya, a foreign-born immigrant knew that, and she did not. Venky said that in 1966 President Johnson had signed the Uniform Time Act, which defined a common Eastern Standard

Time and Eastern Daylight Time. Normally that would have been the end of that, but the US government exempted states that decided to remain on Standard Time. So here Venky had her date and time of birth, but no way of knowing exactly when New Jersey started following Daylight Savings Time. That problem was solved after finding on the Internet positive confirmation that New Jersey had indeed adopted the 1966 law, so that September in 1972 when Tara was born, Daylight Savings was truly in effect. Jaya explained the significance of that datum; Vedic Astrology was based on the positions of celestial objects at a given time in India.

"So what's the verdict," said Tara, annoyed as she saw Venky silently hand over the papers to Jaya.

In a bare whisper, Jaya said, "I see deceit, I see destruction, I see doom, I see despair, I see death."

Tara calmly got up. "You see wrongly. Good night."

ల ల ల ల ల

10:30 p.m., Saturday, August 24, 2002. Tara's residence

It had been quite a strange day, thought Tara as she got into her bed. At noon that day, she had dropped by to see Toby. After making love, they had wanted to get something to eat. *Clams*, he had said, and he knew of a place in Long Branch that served the best clams, so that was where they had to go, but on his motorcycle, with it being a beautiful day. But she was wearing a short skirt, she had protested, and everyone would be able to see her minge.

Yes, but no one will know who you are once you have the helmet on, he had said.

But the cops could pull them over and give her a ticket for indecent exposure, she had said.

Well, I have a get out of jail for free card, he had said with a smile.

Even Catholic girls know how to have fun, she had thought, and had decided to chance it. She had ridden on little Vespas and other assorted two-wheeled put-puts in college, but had never been on a honest-to-goodness high powered motorcycle. She had donned the helmet that he had given her, but could not help wondering how many other girls had done so before her, although it was identical to the one on his head, so there was the possibility that it was just his spare.

He had asked her to put her feet up on the little folding pedals before the motorcycle started to move, and she did that. She had leaned in tightly to him, clumsily clunking her unaccustomed helmet on his. Her arms had naturally wrapped around his waist, her thighs hugging the round of his buttocks. The first thought that had gone through her head was how vulnerable her bare knees were to the cruel macadam; at least he had on blue jeans to protect himself.

Please do not fall, she had implored him, as he had gunned the engine, its meaty *brrrrrappppp* driving unexpected tingles right through her body and rattling her eyeballs. With a mix of excitement and apprehension, she had only shivered and hugged him tighter.

He had ended up dropping the bike, but after they had finished eating, and he was starting it for the trip back home. She had been standing off to one side, busy strapping on her helmet to notice what had actually transpired, and had helped him upright it, which in retrospect seemed unwise. He had seemed quite angry, not only for having let the bike get away from him in the first place, but also for failing to lift it back up himself before Tara had to step in and help out.

A Rainbow of Happiness

Tuesday, Christmas Eve, 2002. Key West, Florida.

"You know I don't have a date," said Tara, shielding the phone against the brisk breeze as she watched the sun set from a balcony in her mother's apartment in Key West. She was certainly being at least partially truthfully, since Toby had to be on extended patrol on New Year's Eve, invariably his busiest and bloodiest night of the entire year.

But even if he was free, she was not interested in revealing her little secret. The unspeakable audacity of her stolen time with him, a quarter of an hour here, a hurried lunch hour there, a prolonged, a wholly unnecessary trip to the grocery store, had certainly spiced up her otherwise lackluster life. Her mother had noticed the little extra bounce in her step, a return of her old joie de vivre, and had only nodded thoughtfully when Tara attributed it to Avakai. com.

"That's why you must come," said Zipper. She had called Tara to remind her about Ramon's big party. "If you need to be that formal, and running out of other options, see if Venky can escort you."

"Venky?"

"Sure, why not? It's not as if you will be on a prom date! It's just a small party of very close friends. Besides, there will be other single guys and gals. Dad knows a lot of people, so you are guaranteed to meet someone who will strike your fancy. Really. Just meet, greet and dance the night away! How can I make it any simpler for you?"

What a swell idea! Tara does Rumson. It must be really nice to live the simple life, thought Tara, noticing how much Zipper sounded just like Tracey. "Sure, and there is a winning New Jersey Lottery ticket waiting for me somewhere too."

"Come on, Tara! Don't be so glum. It's a brand new year coming right up! Ring out the old, ring in the new and all that. You will come as you promised, won't you?"

True, Tara had agreed to attend, when Ramon had asked her during her Thanksgiving party, and also when Zipper had reminded her just before the entire Morgan family had jetted off to Key West for Christmas.

ℰℱ ℰℱ ℰℱ ℰℱ ℰℱ

Tuesday, December 31, 2002. Tara's home.

New Year's Eve had started out worse than Tara had anticipated. She had tossed and turned in bed, wide awake,

246

until shortly after five in the morning. The house was eerily silent and empty, with Jamie and Isabella still in Key West. Her flight home the prior night had been overbooked and late, and the harried crew had run out of all food and beverages except what eventually turned out to be shockingly bad coffee and stale, crumbly, garishly decorated Holiday cookies as they called them. To their credit, the crew had given the passengers two options; delay the departure from Miami by half an hour while they replenished their food supply, or taxi back from the gate that very instant to be third in line for takeoff. The passengers excitedly chose the latter unanimously, but evidently had made no commitment to being understanding about subsequent pangs of hunger during a long flight.

None of that had bothered her, and she had tried to make the best of the situation by reading magazines that she normally only perused at a doctor's office, but a pair of young newlyweds sitting next to her gushed to one another over how life was going to be perfectly wonderful, satisfying and complete, now that they had each other. It wasn't merely a few hurried minutes of highly symbolic tokens of mutual reassurances, but four solid hours of romanticizing and planning every minute detail of their future life together. What had really bothered her was not as much their syrupy promises, but her ire at how the reality of her own quest for a lifelong soul mate had fallen so utterly short of the serious and well-intentioned commitments of her traveling companions. Just about the only thing that she and Todd had ever agreed on during their entire time together was the part where each said I do.

A general despondency in her mood that had thus set in quite early into the flight continued well after she had reached home and climbed wearily into her bed. She had originally planned to have Toby spend the night with her, but somewhere in the dark skies over North Carolina had convinced herself that she would not be good company that night, and called him from the plane to cancel the date, citing exhaustion. To her chagrin, he had unexpectedly acquiesced, too easily she thought, making no attempt whatsoever to plead with her to not cancel their plans, and that vexed her even more.

Tracey was departing for Vail with her family, and had only a precious few distracted moments to talk on the phone; so Tara had to fend for herself for most of the day, emotionally too wounded to call Toby, and growing more wounded with each passing hour. Sometime after a solitary half-eaten lunch of arugula with chunks of bleu cheese drizzled with olive oil, she had fallen asleep in an armchair, snuggled under a light throw.

At precisely five that evening, Toby had called, with ample apologies for not having called sooner. Quite groggy and out of sorts, and with a parched throat and lips, she could only mumble something unintelligible even to herself. He could sneak away during a break at six, he said, if she could see him.

"Do you mind keeping me company while I get dressed?"

"Can I watch?"

"Sure can, but it will cost extra. I'll keep the front door unlocked."

സ സ സ സ സ

Tara was completely dressed and waiting downstairs in the living room by the time Toby drove up in his police cruiser, at 6:45 p.m.

"I need to go to the bathroom," said Tara with a trace of urgency, offering her cheek too briefly even to really notice the frost of his touch as she welcomed him, and hurriedly turning away.

He closed the door clumsily behind him, and took her hand to steady himself, citing many hours of sitting in his cruiser. She reluctantly permitted him to walk her down the corridor, stopping at the large powder room off the living room. Toby was right behind her, his arm wrapped around her hip. He pushed her further into the bathroom, and quickly closed the door before turning on the soft light.

"What are you doing here? I really, really, really need to pee," her voice cracked with urgency and panic.

"Let me watch."

"No! Of course not. Never! Are you crazy?"

"I will watch. I need to."

"You really want to watch me pee?" She bent down and turned on the water to the bidet to warm the water, only then realizing her implied consent.

"Sure! Why not?"

She could certainly recite a litany of very valid reasons why not, mused Tara as she nevertheless reached under her gown and undid the snaps of her lacy garter belt, and pulled down her matching thong. Bunching up the gown around her waist, she sat down on the large toilet seat, the folds of her gown flowing over her arms.

She hoped he would not notice her pale thighs, quite unattractively flattened against the cool seat, and visible above the black thigh-high stockings. The puny inadequacy of her unsteady drizzle was the only sound in the room.

Toby did not say anything, but leaned against the wall in front, his hands in the pockets of his crisply starched uniform, and legs crossed at the ankles, watching her every movement. After she finished, she got up, turned around and hovered over the bidet, her hands still tightly holding her gown out of harm's way while the refreshing arc of warm water cleansed her. Toby handed her an off-white Turkish hand towel from a large wicker basket.

"Thanks. Do you provide this unusually personal level of service for all of your lovers?" She held onto his arm as she stepped off the bidet.

"Only for the most special ones." He drew her closer to him. "Let me see your breasts."

"No, not now! Not here!" Tara stepped back, her Catholic upbringing kicking into high gear. "You really shouldn't even be here!" Did he have a few drinks earlier, she wondered, or maybe partook a bit too carelessly and enthusiastically of the eggnog at the crew lounge at the police station?

"Please." He came still closer. She stepped back, until her derriere grazed the vanity. His breath was warm on her, and was surprisingly devoid of alcohol. "Your breasts look so creamy." His warm palm encircled the cup of her gown, and gently caressed it with one hand. His other hand tenderly massaged the small of her back, somewhat easing her stress and discomfort.

"Not to burst your bubble, but that does absolutely nothing for me," she said, slipping out the words through his moist kiss.

"Which one of my normally irresistible and well-honed techniques is failing to fulfill its intended mission," he asked sternly with a dramatically raised eyebrow.

A cropped mustache would suit him very well, she thought, and traced one on his upper lip with her forefinger. "I really can't feel anything through the reinforced padded bra that is built into this gown."

"Good! Then that's even more reason to remove the offending garment in question, no?" He reached behind her and pulled the zipper down just enough to liberate her breasts, the pink tips of which became the object of his desire and focus. "That's so delicious, so heavenly," he purred. "Did you nurse?"

"Not as much recently, but yes, for eight excruciatingly painful and leaky months. Can you tell?"

"Yes. Your succulent nipples are rightfully plump and juicy, like nice Turkish Sultana raisins. They should be enjoyed more." He stopped abruptly. "But my neck is getting sore." He helped her ease her butt onto the vanity. She splayed her knees out and welcomed him closer, her arms clasped around his neck. "You must lose the handcuffs and the heat first, Rambo."

"Maybe I should follow you to your party," he said, "with my sirens blaring, lights flashing, to arrest you, truss you and take you into my protective custody."

"You forgot to mention your truncheon swinging. Where will you take me, to your Turkish prison? My, I leave you alone for ten days and you turn into quite an alpha dog in heat. I should do this more often."

He undid the buckle to the holster and lowered it until his sidearm clinked on the marble floor, followed by the hand-cuffs, flashlight and radio. "Now where were we again?"

"You got me all hot and flustered and bothered and I have a party to go to that I really don't want to, so just hurry up and stick it in and swirl it around. That's where we are, pal. What's the delay here? Nothing more to see here, so let's move it, move it, move it!"

Toby dropped his pants, and Tara closed her eyes and leaned back lightly, bathed in warm, tingly anticipation. A few seconds later, she became acutely aware that not much seemed to be happening. "How ya doin' below decks, sailor?" she asked teasingly. Reaching down, she realized that although not quite a wet noodle, he was certainly not going in without a struggle. In an attempt to try and quickly revive the situation at hand, she bent down, but Toby brusquely brushed her away and turned to pull his pants up.

"What's the matter, Toby? Did I do something wrong?" she asked plaintively. "Toby, what is the matter? Answer me!"

He shook his head grimly, punctuating his finality by strapping on his regulation issued accoutrement. The look on his face was one of total anguish, and he did not have to say anything.

Tara sat up in shock as the chilling realization set in. His cancer was finally beginning to ravage his entire body, especially in the inevitable way he had warned her it would. That also explained the unsteadiness when he had first walked into the house. "I really don't have to go to the party...."

"But I have to report back to duty," he said, cutting her off very firmly, his arms defiantly akimbo, but his eyes betraying his innermost torment even as they avoided her intense scrutiny.

She could not resist the onslaught of panic grabbing hold of her senses. She held on to her cheeks with her hands to prevent throwing up, and then took a couple of deep, loud breaths through her cupped fingers, suddenly acutely fearful of him doing something unmentionably devastating. "Please promise me that you will come back here as soon as you possibly can? Tonight? Please, Toby? Please?"

"Tara, look. Going into this we agreed it wouldn't be a serious relationship."

Tara slid off the vanity and stood up in a hurry. Even as she asked him why she should not hurt when her best friend hurts, another part of her was questioning who would keep their best friend a well-kept secret? "Come with me. Call in sick," she said in a burst of reckless abandon, yet cringing internally at the incongruity of her own last statement.

She reached out for his hand, which he took. For that alone, she was very grateful, and more so when he unexpectedly raised it, however fleetingly, to his lips. As she tried to pull him closer, he resisted, but not before she noticed that he had lost all of his love-handles in just two weeks. Although he said that he would see her after the end of his shift, it struck her as being mechanical and not at all convincing. With that, he turned around and walked out into the cold with a firm step.

 барбарбарбарбар

9:45 p.m., New Years' Eve. The DiCastro residence. Rumson.

It wasn't just a small party of very close friends, by any stretch of the imagination. Tara estimated there were over four hundred people at the DiCastro's affair that night. Her first clue as to its extravagance was the long Conga line of very expensive chauffeur-driven luxury cars that pulled into the massive circular driveway that wrapped around a breathtaking, brilliantly lit fountain that sprayed scented water high into the air, with swirling, wispy plumes at the top that magically disappeared into the cold night. There were young, energetic and courteous valets in crisp uniforms and shellacked hair to assist the less fortunate who had to drive themselves. There was even a large, snow white tent set up to store their coats. Those in chauffeured cars had no need for coats. Their rides would be held awaiting, steady to within a degree of their preferred temperature.

She had arrived there by herself, even though Venky had offered her a ride. As luck would have it, he had arrived at almost the same time, and he spotted her first, and waved. She had expected him to be accompanied, and was mildly disappointed to see him there by himself. His sister Jaya had arrived earlier, he said, with a few others. He sheepishly apologized for not wearing a tuxedo. He didn't own one, he said, and could not bear the thought of wearing a rented one. But Tara thought that the elegant dark suit he had on, with a crisply starched white shirt and a dark tie, was fine.

The house, although very wide, had little in the way of remarkable architectural details, and appeared to be mostly a single-storied row of very tall, thin, floor to ceiling windows, separated by equal widths of stone walls. A parapet wall ran around the entire perimeter of the roof, and behind it she could see parts of building structures. As they entered the house, Tara noticed that the entrance foyer, and that was a very loose description of the panorama that commanded her attention, was in reality an open interior bridge that drew her eyes to a large bubble of an elevator at the far end of the house. To their immediate left and right were two giant, sweeping arcs of a circular staircase that echoed the circular driveway, and one led down to the lower level, whereas the other led upstairs. Save for the elevator, the far end appeared to be a wall of glass.

"Oh my God!" said Tara, a burst of dizziness causing her to hold on to Venky's arm. A young lady in a black dress welcomed them, and said that the entire house was open, save for the family wing, and that they could go anywhere. The DiCastros were mingling, she said, and her recommendation was to take the elevator all the way down, and work their way up.

By now completely lightheaded, Tara barely paid attention to Venky's calling out various details to her attention as they took the elevator to the lowest level. The elevator itself was a glass cocoon that traveled outside the house, offering a bird's eye view of the house and the Shrewsbury River that separated it from the town of Sea Bright, nestled on the slender barrier island that in turn separated it from the Atlantic Ocean. They descended more than four levels before stopping only ten or so feet above sea level. Surrounding them was a well-lit pool, half of which was underneath the house, which was supported by wide concrete pillars, and the other half cantilevered out past the riverbank. A staircase led down to the riverfront, where a dock secured a huge motor yacht, a sailboat and a couple of wave runners.

Quite a few youngsters were in the pool, which most certainly heated. There were showers, and baskets abounded, some of neatly folded towels, and others of swimsuits emblazoned with the logo Rodenberg, LLP. What a novel solution, thought Tara, to the problem of guests showing up without swimwear.

The next level up turned out to be a 25-seat private movie theater with its own stage, and the movie South Pacific was being screened.

Above the theater was office space, with half a dozen display tables showcasing detailed architectural models of huge real estate developments, some of which Tara recognized right away. One, which Tara knew that had not been built yet, depicted the development of a narrow, urban tract along the Jersey Shore in Asbury Park. Tara had a feeling that a lot of eminent domain issues of urban blight were at stake on that project.

The next level was off limits, and Tara surmised that it was the DiCastro's living quarters. Venky and Tara got off one level lower than where they had originally started, spotted Zipper, and went over to greet her.

"I'm glad that you are here," said Zipper, planting a genuine kiss on her cheek and embracing her tightly before greeting Venky. Zipper wore a sleeveless and backless black silk dress that arched up in front to a point at her throat, with a band that circled around her neck, and formed a bowtie at the front. Her normally wavy and curly hair was smooth, and brushed back. Tara had never seen her with heels before, and added to her natural height, Zipper stood slightly over six feet. Her makeup was exquisite, and so far removed from her normal indifference that Tara was left speechless.

"You just missed the Governor of New Jersey," Zipper said nonchalantly. "He stopped by to say hi before heading back to Drumthwacket," which was his official residence, in Princeton. "Dad is such an ardent fan of his," she said by way of explanation, as if that was the ticket to such a visit, as she walked them over to the food. Zipper cradled two plates on her arm and personally ladled various delicacies on them like herbed grouse terrine with truffles, and foie gras. She handed them to Tara and Venky before preparing a small plate for herself to keep them company.

"We follow Kashrut," said Zipper, referring to the Jewish dietary laws, so there would be no mixing of meat and dairy dishes, nor non-kosher meats such as pork, nor shellfish. As they finished nibbling at their food, Zipper said that a band was playing upstairs, with a lot of dancing, and their colleagues from Avakai were already up there. As Venky turned to respond to someone's casual comment, Zipper whispered to Tara that her dad specifically wanted to show Tara around the rest of the house, and that she would look after Venky.

11:15 p.m., New Year's Eve. Ramon DiCastro's Private Study. Rumson.

"When Debora Rodenberg and I married," said Ramon as they sat in his study, sipping champagne from small flutes, "her parents owned a small construction firm in Red Bank." He waved an unlit Cuban cigar at his opulent surroundings. "We had none of these trappings. In fact we didn't have two dimes to rub together. I was fresh out of law school, and the Rodenbergs had not figured out how to break into the construction business here."

"So what's your secret," asked Tara, truthfully impressed with his demonstrated success, and took a sip of her champagne as she casually looked around, wondering where Debora was, since she had not even met her yet.

"I became a consigliere," he said.

Tara almost choked on her drink. "Consigliere? Like in an advisor to a mafia don?" She had seen The Godfather movie at least half a dozen times.

Ramon laughed easily. "Mario Puzo didn't have it quite right," he said with a dismissive wave of his hand. "A consigliere is simply an advisor to a wealthy family. In my case it was to a very wealthy dowager of Sicilian roots, but an honest, upright, Catholic woman who had a unique way of getting people to part with their property."

Tara raised an eyebrow. This was getting quite interesting. "I'm not going to ask if she sent over decapitated mare's heads, Ramon. I truly won't, honest!" she said with a look of deliberately contrived sincerity.

"Well, you just did," he said with a broad smile. "Keep in mind that many of the local landowners were pensioners of Italian descent. She would go to their houses dressed in black, with baskets of fresh homemade Italian pastries like Cannolis, rum-soaked Babalones, Napoleons, Sfogliatelles and Tira Misus, but she would carefully and elaborately hand them over one little morsel of pastry at a time, and show them brochures of Florida real estate, and she would talk longingly of the warm sun, the blue water, the golden sand, and of course the absence of snow and ice." Ramon smiled in fond memory. "She could only speak English, but she would memorize as many Italian words as she could, and sprinkle them liberally throughout her conversation. This old lady could work those pensioners over in her sleep."

He had real estate licenses in New Jersey and Florida, Ramon said. So he made money on both transactions, and the dowager put up the money to buy the properties in New Jersey. "She used every single sale to convince the surrounding neighbors to move along with their buddies," said Ramon. Older Italians like to be surrounded by other paisanos, so that helped." The Rodenbergs were then hired to remodel the houses, and when the dowager flipped the renovated houses, Ramon would profit from the transaction yet again.

"That must have been such a sweet deal," said Tara, shaking her head in amazement.

"Exactly," he smiled, looking at his watch. "So in the end we all made out well." With exactly ten minutes remaining until midnight, they made their way upstairs to join the rest.

ფ ფ ფ ფ ფ

1:00 a.m., New Years' Day. The DiCastro residence. Rumson.

With Toby weighing heavily on her mind, in spite of, or perhaps because of, the gaiety around her, Tara stayed on the sidelines while the dancing was still going strong on the open rooftop. She had patiently waited until that time to try and leave without appearing to be rude. Ramon and

Debora were nowhere to be found, and as she bade her farewell to Zipper, Venky gallantly offered to escort her downstairs.

As they waited for a valet to pull up her car, they walked up to the fountain, which was still going pretty strong in spite of the cold. A fog continuously rose from the waters, and was quickly dissipated by the wind.

"When I was growing up in India," said Venky, a hint of nostalgia in his voice, "we used to toss a make a wish and toss a coin into water." He dug into his pocket and pulled out a couple of quarters, giving one to Tara.

As she prepared to toss hers, Venky turned around, his back to the water. "The idea is that you do not see what is happening. That way, even if you miss, you do not feel bad."

Tara smiled. "OK, let's do it your way. But it's a rather big fountain, so we won't miss, will we?"

Venky glanced at her, and said patiently "You are supposed to keep your eyes closed. Perfect. On the count of three we toss the coin over our right shoulder."

Two satisfying plinks signaled their success.

"Everyone has a big rainbow of happiness with their name on it," said Venky, "and I am blessed to have found mine.

My wish was that all of my friends and family would find theirs."

A big rainbow of happiness with my name on it is exactly what I need right now, thought Tara, looking up wistfully at the dark sky, the first of the New Year. Who knew what it had in store? Had Venky read that line somewhere or had he come up with it on his own, she wondered. Nevertheless, that sentiment most definitely buoyed up her spirits, she conceded.

"What was your wish, Tara?"

That shocked her back into reality. "It's my secret, mine to keep!"

Venky earnestly shook his head. "Of course not. Otherwise people could make really evil wishes! The only way to keep that from happening is for the person making the wish to announce it. Isn't that how you do it?"

"No," she said, never having heard of that rule. "What happens if you make one wish and announce another?"

He had that angle covered. "Well, lore has it that then both the wishes announced and secret will cancel each other out, and you will get neither!"

"No way! That can't be!" protested Tara, alarmed. "No, you don't understand. It was a very, very deeply and intensely personal wish! I can't reveal it to you!"

Venky raised his hands, palms out. "What can I say? I didn't make the rules! Do you want your wish to come true or not?"

"I so desperately want it to come true," said Tara. So desperately, her heart ached with every beat. She could tell by the look on Venky's face that he realized it was very true. That she shared her sentiment so easily with Venky surprised herself, even though he had always been very approachable and receptive to heartfelt discussions. Emboldened, Tara took a deep breath and decided to throw all caution to the wind. "Look, if I tell you exactly what I wished for, do you promise not to ever reveal it to anyone? Never, ever?" This was turning out to be a night of promises, Tara thought. Would they be ever kept? "All I wish for", said Tara softly, "is that I can carry someone's child." There was of course another wish that she desired more than anything else; Toby surviving his deadly cancer. But deep in her heart she knew that it was sadly way beyond reach. So she had opted for the next best thing. Having said that, she felt no mortification at all in sharing such an intimate thought with a coworker, but instead a wave of euphoria washed over her. She had hardly been drinking, save for a half of the small flute of champagne in Ramon's study, and a token sip of another at midnight; so it was not the liquor talking, as far as she could tell. If she had not suffered an early miscarriage on Memorial Day, she would have been almost 7 months in gestation.

Her blurted desire did not seem to faze him at all. The expression on his face was not one of voyeuristic satisfaction, but one of a genuine understanding acceptance, which she found curiously intriguing. "Someone's? Anyone's?" he asked.

Tara had to laugh out at that. "A very special someone in particular."

"I am certainly not a doctor," he said with a straight face, "and I have never played one on TV either. But people have often mistaken me for being one, so that qualifies me to give you advice. Have you tried sex? Usually that seems to work, at least for unwed teenagers."

"Usually that does appear to be the case, yes. But..." she drew the line right there. "This is getting way too personal, Venky."

"Ah, yes, you are quite right." Venky reached out as to shake her hand. "Anyway, for whatever it's worth, my wish was that your wish will come true. More so than mine."

Still firmly grasping her hand, he looked her in the eyes and said, "I will safeguard your thoughts, and not share them with anyone."

Even though she was sure he would not blab her juicy secrets, hearing him say that made her glad that she had confided in him. She gave him a quick kiss on his cheek, catching him completely by surprise. "Happy 2003 to you too."

The Incredible Darkness of Yearning

11:55 p.m., Sunday night, Jan 5, 2003. Tara's home. Middletown.

Tara huddled on the floor in a corner of Jamie's room, a glass of chilled vodka at her side. All the lights were off, save a small nightlight tucked away between the headboard and the wall. With Jamie and Isabella still in Key West, Tara had kept the thermostat quite low, in spite of the wintry bluster outside. She swabbed at her teary eyes with a hand towel, hastily grabbed from Jamie's bathroom, squeezing herself tightly into the corner walls. She tugged on the hood of the sweatshirt, worn to stave off the cold, pulling it as far forward as the garment allowed her, shielding her face and the unspeakable anguish behind it from God, for at that time she truly felt utterly betrayed.

Earlier that evening, even if the young lady on the phone had not announced herself as Toby Roland's younger sister Jody, Tara would have had absolutely no problem discerning the strong genetic link in her voice, masked though it was by shock and emotion. Toby had fallen and struck his head on one of the cleats on his boat, Jody had informed her.

269

"Sorry, the doctor's looking for me. I must go now," Jody had said urgently, hanging up before Tara could even volunteer her help. Was Toby even alive at that point? Where was he? Could she see him?

Tara had immediately dialed the Riverview Medical Center, which was on her speed dial, for Jamie's sake. When Tara had asked the receptionist to be connected to a new patient, Toby Roland, she was not told that no such patient had been admitted, so Tara had surmised that he had to be there. To the question *are you a relative* Tara had responded *no*, and had been informed that she could not be put through.

Shortly before noon of that same day, Tara had spoken to Toby, after he had just returned from an overnight shift. They had spoken for about ten minutes, and she had promised to see him for dinner in exchange for his promise to go straight to bed. It will be hard, he had chuckled at his double entendre, to fall asleep in anticipation of her arrival.

Don't stay up watching TV, she had admonished him.

Scarcely half an hour later, she had driven to the marina, wearing absolutely nothing but a long woolen double-breasted winter coat buttoned all the way up to her neck, and leather boots. As she had pulled in to the parking lot, the sight of a red Aston Martin roadster, deliberately parked at an angle to take up two slots in an otherwise empty lot, had caused her to turn right around and hightail it back out, stopping on a side street out of sight. Getting out of her car, she saw Toby out on the back of his boat, talking to a unmistakable, tall, chatty blonde. Without taking her eyes off them, Tara dug out her cell phone and dialed Tracey's cell phone. Her heart sinking, hoping wildly that her own eyes were blatantly lying to her, she watched the woman reach into her purse, only to shake her head and zip it back up. Then, the woman reached up to Toby and there was no mistaking the familiarity, intent and intimacy of their gestures towards each other. She could tell that this was certainly no innocent, chance encounter on the street for the two. But just how long had Tracey been sleeping with Toby?

Distraught as she was, Tara admitted to herself that the only sin of which Tracey was guilty was adultery, pure and simple. Even though she hadn't caught them interlocked in bed *flagrante delicto* as she had her husband Todd, there was no doubt in her mind that it was not an innocent, platonic hello that she had witnessed being exchanged on the aft deck of the boar. Besides, even at the most sympathetic level, even unconsummated lust in the heart was morally equivalent to adultery, as she had been taught. As far as

Tara was concerned Tracey had cheated on her husband, Walter, and that was the end of their relationship.

Tara had not confided to anyone about her relationship with Toby, and at that point it was pure conjecture on her part as to whether Toby had leaked it to Tracey or not. Had they lain in post-coital haze, chuckling over how they had pulled the wool over each other's partner, toasting their cunning?

The absurdity of the whole situation churned in her over-wrought mind. One the one hand, here she was, not only faced with the vast uncertainty of his spreading illness, but also of the shocking revelation of his infidelity, and then to top it all, his sudden coma. On the other hand, Tara agonized over whether it was possible for her to bemoan the loss of something that she may have never possessed in the first place? Having had purposely kept Toby out of her social life, what claim could she now pull out of her pocket and enforce on him, and under what authority? After almost a year together, clearly they were little more than each other's toy, to be pulled out at whim, held and played with, and hastily crammed back into the toy box at the end of the day. But, he was still her toy, wasn't he, and exactly who was Tracey to sneak into her toy box and slyly enjoy her toy?

❧ ❧ ❧ ❧ ❧

9:20 a.m., Monday, Jan 6, 2003. Tara's home. Middletown, NJ.

It was Jody who called Tara. Apparently neither had slept that night. Jody's speech was halting and sometimes incoherent, and the connection was full of static, but Tara discerned that Toby's brain was still continuing to swell, although not as rapidly as it had been at first, and that during the night, he had been airlifted in a helicopter to the University of Pennsylvania's Level 1 Trauma Center. There, the doctors were putting him into an induced coma, to reduce the intracranial pressure. It was possible, Jody said, that after coming out of the coma Toby might have cognitive impairment, but there was no other choice. Much as she wanted to scream out the question, Tara refrained from asking Jody who had called 911.

The final call came from Jody at 6 p.m. that evening. Toby had just died.

❧ ❧ ❧ ❧ ❧

1:45 p.m. Saturday, Jan 11, 2003. Mill Run, Pennsylvania.

Tara drove fast on the way back from Toby's funeral, which kept her deliberately focused on the road. The deep, drawn, low frequency church bells that had pelted out their mournful *dooooooommmmmm, dooooooommmmmm, dooooooommmmmm* still resonated through every bone in her body, and the liturgy of the Requiem Mass gave her the shivers.

Requiem aeternam dona eis, Domine

Grant them eternal rest, Lord,

et lux perpetua luceat eis.

And let perpetual light shine on them.

She reminisced about that time very early in their relationship, when Toby had said that he only had a limited time for anger, and had all eternity to think about regrets.

She looked up briefly at the brilliant blue sky, tears again running down her face. Toby, I sincerely hope that you do not have any regrets. I understand that there were certain things that you felt that you had to do in the awfully short time that God had let you walk amongst us. Please do not regret that you may have hurt me, since I forgive you for giving in to your temptations. Hear my prayer, dear Lord, and please grant Toby his eternal rest.

Her jaw clenched tight in deep anger as she acknowledged that while he could now sleep as an innocent, that certainly did not in any way diminish or excuse Tracey's marital malfeasance.

She had arrived by herself the prior evening after a 6-hour drive with scant traffic, and had attended the last viewing of Toby Roland. Her tears had flowed well before that time, and the deep throbbing of her head helped her to keep her composure as she had knelt before his open casket.

Immediately thereafter, she had met Toby's immediate family; his younger sister Jody, his parents Frank and Matilda, and scores of assorted uncles, aunts, cousins and close friends. Even though she and Toby had talked frequently about his family, neither had broached the idea of her ever meeting them. She had belatedly realized, with considerable chagrin, that she had no clue whatsoever of how Toby had explained their relationship, or even if he had at all.

Jody, buried as she was in her immeasurable grief, had extracted a dogeared sheet of paper and shown it to Tara. It was a handwritten card that she herself had never seen, from Jamie, to Toby. On one side of the card was the outline of a bunch of red, blue, yellow and green balloons, all tied together. On the flip side, it read:

Dear Officer Toby,

Hope you become well.

Love, Jamie

"Please let me keep this," Jody had requested, "it meant so much to my brother."

How terrible it must be for a mother, thought Tara, to be burying her child. The Stations of the Cross! That was why he would not accompany her to the celebration of one of the most poignant services of the Catholic Church! It was not that he feared own death; it was that he dreaded the thought of his mother having to bury him!

That night, Tara opened a sealed envelope that Jody had given her, specifically requesting that she not read it until later.

The Sum of All Fears

Dearest Tara,

As an infant, I feared the absence of my mother.

As a toddler, I feared the unfamiliar.

As a child, I feared monsters, ghosts and goblins.

As a student, I feared incomprehension.

As an adolescent, I feared rejection.

As a soldier, I feared cowardice.

As a friend, I feared betrayal.

As a neighbor, I feared loss of face.

As a worker, I feared incompetence.

As a parishioner, I feared faithlessness.

As a lover, I feared inadequacy.

As a spouse, I feared infidelity.

As a parent, I feared the loss of a child.

As a retiree, I feared uncertainty.

As I prepare for my final sleep,

I fathom that all my life,

I have feared fear,

and have succumbed to its tyranny.

I no longer fear.

Eternally yours,

Toby Roland

P.S. I fear I did not get past the 'lover' stage, but I sure tried mighty hard.

The End of The Awakening